P9-BZO-323

HOT UNDER THE COLLAR

The fire was starting to spread as Ranger Sergeant Woodward poked his head and a Colt up through the ladder trap. He told the only man there to drop his six-gun.

Longarm did as he was told; he was no fool. But as he stood there amid the swirling gun smoke, he called out, "This is a hell of a time for formalities, Sarge! I'm on your side and this place seems to be on fire. Let me show you my badge and I'll help you haul these bodies out of here. I doubt your fire volunteers will arrive soon enough to do much good."

But the ranger insisted, "You just stay put while I climb on up for a better look at you, stranger. Anyone can *say* he's the famous Longarm. You're going to have to convince me some."

DON'T MISS THESE
ALL-ACTION WESTERN SERIES
FROM THE BERKLEY PUBLISHING GROUP

THE GUNSMITH by J. R. Roberts
Clint Adams was a legend among lawmen, outlaws, and ladies.
They called him . . . the Gunsmith.

LONGARM by Tabor Evans
The popular long-running series about U.S. Deputy Marshal
Long—his life, his loves, his fight for justice.

SLOCUM by Jake Logan
Today's longest-running action Western. John Slocum rides
a deadly trail of hot blood and cold steel.

BUSHWHACKERS by B. J. Lanagan
An action-packed series by the creators of Longarm! The
rousing adventures of the most brutal gang of cutthroats ever
assembled—Quantrill's Raiders.

DIAMONDBACK by Guy Brewer
Dex Yancey is Diamondback, a southern gentleman turned
con man when his brother cheats him out of the family fortune. Ladies love him. Gamblers hate him. But nobody pulls
one over on Dex . . .

WILDGUN by Jack Hanson
Will Barlow's continuing search for his daughter, kidnapped
by the Blackfeet Indians who slaughtered the rest of his family.

TABOR EVANS

LONGARM

AND THE
TEXAS TIGER LADY

JOVE BOOKS, NEW YORK

If you purchased this book without a cover, you should be aware that this book is stolen property. It was reported as "unsold and destroyed" to the publisher and neither the author nor the publisher has received any payment for this "stripped book."

This is a work of fiction. Names, characters, places, and incidents are either the product of the author's imagination or are used fictitiously, and any resemblance to actual persons, living or dead, business establishments, events, or locales is entirely coincidental.

LONGARM AND THE TEXAS TIGER LADY

A Jove Book / published by arrangement with
the author

PRINTING HISTORY
Jove edition / August 2001

All rights reserved.
Copyright © 2001 by Penguin Putnam Inc.
This book, or parts thereof, may not be reproduced in any form
without permission.
For information address: The Berkley Publishing Group,
a division of Penguin Putnam Inc.,
375 Hudson Street, New York, New York 10014.

The Penguin Putnam Inc. World Wide Web site address is
www.penguinputnam.com

ISBN: 0-515-13117-2

A JOVE BOOK®
Jove Books are published by The Berkley Publishing Group,
a division of Penguin Putnam Inc.,
375 Hudson Street, New York, New York 10014.
JOVE and the "J" design
are trademarks belonging to Penguin Putnam Inc.

PRINTED IN THE UNITED STATES OF AMERICA

10 9 8 7 6 5 4 3 2 1

Chapter 1

There were times to stand your ground, times to walk away, and times to run like hell. So Deputy U.S. Marshal Custis Long of the Denver District Court took a running dive into a glorious sunset by way of the front window of the Silverheels Saloon to land on a shoulder and roll across the plank walk as shattered glass spun down like frosted maple leaves. He rolled off the far edge of the walk and slithered backward under the sun-silvered and glass-strewn planks like a sidewinder, dusting the front of his tobacco tweed suit considerably, and he knew he had more crawling by far ahead of him.

But he lay doggo under the walk for the moment as, sure enough, a whole lot of boot heels thudded out of the saloon to crunch busted glass as they slowed to a thoughtful shuffle. Then somebody up yonder declared, "He's run clean out of sight with his tail betwixt his legs and who'd have ever thought it!"

Another voice declared in a jovial tone, "You done it, Solitaire! You crawfished the famous Longarm! He was afraid to fight you in spite of his rep! But I don't mind telling you I'm surprised as hell, too!"

A voice the lawman under their feet recognized as that of Solitaire Stryker, wanted federal on many a flier, tried to sound modest as it declared, "There was never a pony that couldn't be rode, and Longarm's rep sounded too good to be true. They say that for all his brag, Wild Bill Hickok backed down from Wes Hardin that time, too."

An older and hence possibly wiser voice declared, "I can't see shit across the way with the sun so low and the shadows so long. I vote we go on after him or duck back inside. For anyone can see he could be standing bold as brass in the shade of that far side and he *did* have a double action .44-40 on him, Solitaire!"

The federal want who'd just challenged a lone lawman in a saloon full of his own kind snorted in derision to opine, "You all heard me tell him to fill his fist or git. You all saw him git so fast he missed the front door entire! Far be it for this old boy to compare hisself to old John Wesley Hardin, but both of us have managed to prove that once you gun your *first* famous lawman none of the *other* famous lawmen care to mess with you."

The voice who seemed less easy about standing on busted glass in full sunlight volunteered, "I'll drink to that," and the whole bunch of say eight or ten crunched back inside to belly up to the bar in honor of a suddenly more famous Solitaire Stryker.

Longarm, as he was better known around the Denver District Court, was only under them as they commenced the festivities. The crawlspace under the Silverheels Saloon allowed him to make better time on his hands and knees, once he was in a ways from the front walk. The frame building had been jerry built on cedar posts without digging a caller and some of the original prairie sod was still in place, dried to where it was as dusty but cleaner than the bare 'dobe and horseshit of the street out front.

In the taproom above, as Longarm had hoped, Solitaire Stryker was commencing to reconsider his previous plans for an evening in the less respectable Denver neighborhoods south of Cherry Creek. He'd meant it when he'd called that tall, tanned lawman's bluff, just now. He hadn't had any choice. When an owlhoot rider was wanted on more than one federal murder warrant, he had nothing to gain by coming along quiet.

So getting it over with in the most desperate gunfight had a public hanging beat by many a mile. But now that the shock was wearing off, the killer was finding it tougher by the minute to hold the glass in his hand steady enough to keep from spilling booze on his boots. For, if the truth were to be told, Solitaire Stryker was numbly surprised to find himself still alive. They'd told him Longarm was the real thing. Stryker had been fixing to crap his britches when it had been Longarm who'd cut and run instead!

But now that Longarm had, the federal want who'd won that hand had to consider the next deal as the cards were still ashuffle. If Longarm had turned out yellow, he was still a federal lawman and Denver, all of it, was still his town. So, whilst it sure felt swell to drink with old boys who patted him on the back and sung his praises, that tall drink of water in the tobacco tweed suit, coffee-brown Stetson and stovepipe boots had less than a mile to run for all the help he needed to back even a yellow-belly's play.

Lest any of his rougher pals wonder about the color of his own belly, Solitaire Stryker never said he was lighting out for the railroad yards. He said he had to take a leak and left a glass half full on the bar as silent proof of his intention to return. Then he strode out the back door toward the shithouse in the backyard. He glanced back, saw he seemed to have the heavily shaded rear of the saloon all to himself under a crimson and lavender sky, and strode on past the shithouse for the alley gate. As he did so something cold and hard poked into the small of his back as Longarm told him, calmly, "Just raise your hands shoulder-high as you keep walking for that alley gate, old son. I don't give such breaks to your kind, often. But they ordered me to bring you in alive, if I could. So let's just see if I can. You can lower your left hand to open that gate as soon as I relieve you of this Schofield .45-Short. How come a rider who brags on being such a mankiller packs such a sissy weapon, Solitaire?"

As the owlhoot rider felt his holster empty he managed to bluster, "I reckon if a U.S. Cavalry round is good enough for Mister Lo, the Poor Indian, it's good enough for a pissant with a badge!"

Longarm said, "Open the gate. I'm too scared. Turn right when we hit the alley. Your pals will have expected me to frog-march you toward the Larimer Street bridge, once they notice you're missing. I fear that, thanks to you, it's going to take me some pistol whupping in this part of town to enjoy some respect again."

"You don't deserve no respect! You fight dirty!" griped the prisoner Longarm was herding south along the alley at gunpoint, now.

Longarm chuckled fondly and replied, not unkindly, "Where in the U.S. Constitution does it say a lawman has to be *fair* to an infernal *outlaw*? My orders were to take you alive, if possible, in any manner possible. When one of my own secret pals around the Larimer Steet Arcade told me you were hanging out in the Silverheels with a rough crowd I knew of old, I figured they'd stay out of it if you'd come quiet. How come you got 'em all het up by acting like such a total asshole, just now?"

Stryker modestly replied, "I wasn't the one who dove

4

headfirst out the front window. I'll thank you to remember I stood my ground and told you I'd as soon fight as surrender like a sissy! Can I put my hands down, now, seeing you got my gun?"

Longarm replied, not unkindly, "Your hands will do just fine where they are. We know about the derringer in your right boot and the bowie in the left. Once I get you over to some brighter streetlamps and at least one other lawman to cover you whilst I pat you down, you can put your fool hands in your pockets for all I care."

"My arms are commencing to ache. I ain't used to walking so fast with my hands like so, damn it!" Stryker protested.

So Longarm said, "Bueno. Stop where you are and put your hands behind you, then. I might have known a man who's never done an honest day's work in his life would have delicate feelings."

As Stryker felt the cold steel of Longarm's handcuffs snap snuggly around his wrists he protested, "Hold on! I never said I wanted to be chained like an animal!"

Longarm poked him in the floating ribs to reply, "Let's move it on out. At the risk of insulting mad dogs, you *are* an animal. A *dumb* animal. You could have come quiet back there and saved the saloon a heap of window glass. I fear I may have to get this outfit dry-cleaned, too. They've been so fussy about the way we dress around the federal building since old Rutherford B. got elected on that fool reform ticket. I want you to swing left at the next cinder footpath betwixt them dark frames ahead. One's a carriage house and the other house is haunted, to hear the neighborhood kids talk. We're going to cross Cherry Creek the informal way. The water's barely ankle-deep betwixt the sandbars and it's mostly sandbars, this late in the summer."

"Durn it, I paid good money for these tooled Mex boots," protested Stryker.

Longarm soothed, "Boots worth shit ought to get you across with dry socks, then. These old army boots are inclined to leak a mite, but it can't be helped when I spend so much time tracking you rascals around on foot. A heap of you run. So I have to chase after you in well broken-in boots with low heels. I'm sure you noticed, just now, how fast I was able to move on my feet when I saw I had to either kill you or run away from you."

"You moved like spit on a hot stove!" sighed the handcuffed man out ahead, adding, "Where in thunder did you run off to after you dove out the front way? We were right behind you. But you were out of sight by the time we made it out front!"

Longarm explained, "I rolled off the edge and crawled under you all to that shithouse I was waiting behind. I didn't wait *inside* the same lest somebody else come out ahead of you on a more innocent errand. I knew you'd come out alone, sooner or later. They don't call you Solitaire because you hold hands with other kids in the dark. So consider how far ahead of you I was thinking and tell me some more about assholes."

"All right, you slickered me," Stryker grudgingly replied. Then he asked in a surprisingly conversational tone, "How come you went to all this trouble to take me alive, Longarm? When you came through them batwing doors and one of the boys whispered who you were, I was sure my life was over, but resolved to end it like a man. When I dared you to slap leather back there, the last thing I was expecting was for things to turn out this way! You don't exactly have a rep for kindness and mercy, you know."

The light was getting tricky. Longarm could make out the gleam of streetlamps on sluggishy moving leadfoil

6

as they strolled through a weed-filled expanse toward the reedy south bank of Cherry Creek, about a furlong across and mayhaps two inches deep where any water ran at all.

In reply to his prisoner's question, Longarm explained, "You hadn't ought to believe everything they print about me in the *Post* and *Rocky Mountain News*, old son. If I have any rep I pride myself on, it's for carrying out my orders as tight as fate and you muley sons of bitches will allow. I've never gunned a want I could have brung in alive. But as you just now proved, a heap of wants don't want to listen to sweet reason and for a minute, back there, I was really afraid you were done for. But my boss, Marshal Billy Vail, laid particular stress on them wanting me to bring you back alive. So move it on out and let's see how wet our socks wind up if we hopscotch some across them sandbars."

As they forged through the reeds Longarm added, "Watch your step. It ain't true there's quicksand along Cherry Creek, but you can mire down a ways in some spots. They keep talking about masonry embankments through the center of town, but I'll believe it when I see it and, by the way, don't give in to the temptation to bolt as we approach the far bank. I told my boss I'd *try* to bring you back alive. I never promised not to bring you in with shot-up shinbones."

Stryker whined, "If I could count on you killing me clean I'd tell you what to do to your mother and just start running. You know they're fixing to hang me. So why are they being so picky about the shape I'm in when you haul me before the judge?"

Longarm answered honestly, "Beats the shit out of me. I never gave the orders. I'm only trying to carry 'em out. Mayhaps they want to talk to you about your wicked past before they stretch your wicked neck. All I know is they asked me not to kill you unless I had to. So I have no

7

call to kill a handcuffed man when a bullet in his leg will calm him down just as well."

There was no arguing with such logic. So it was barely dark out by the time Longarm had Solitaire Stryker locked away for the night in a patent cell at the Federal House Of Detention betwixt the Union Station and the Federal Building closer to Broadway, leaving Longarm free for the night in the company of a certain young widow woman up on Capitol Hill.

As the trail song went, she was young and pretty, too, and had what they called her ring-dang-doo. So a grand night was had by all and then, as all things good and bad must end, she'd served him breakfast in bed with a French lesson and it was time to get on over to his more tedious chores at the infernal Federal Building.

Longarm tried not to get there too early, lest he wipe that smug smile off old Henry, the young squirt who played the typewriter just inside the oaken door lettered U.S. MARSHAL WILLIAM VAIL in gold leaf. But thanks to his having to slip out of that certain brownstone mansion's back gate before the fashionable ladies along the rim of the so-called Capitol Hill, which was really a mesa, were up and about, he showed up at the office early enough to startle their clerk-typist a mite.

Old Henry would have made a dreadful poker player, but he tried to keep a straight face as he told Longarm, "It's a good thing for you that you made it before the boss sent a posse out after you. He told me to send you back the moment you got in."

So Longarm ambled on back to the oak-paneled inner sanctum of Billy Vail, as he was more commonly known in the flesh. Longarm lit one of his three-for-a-nickel cheroots along the way in self-defense. It still made his eyes water a mite as he entered the smoke-filled and seldom aired-out lair of his somewhat older and way shorter and

8

stockier boss. For those black stogies old Billy smoked constantly never ceased to amaze everyone around him, as the marshal somehow managed to stay alive with his head in such a pungent cloud.

As Longarm entered, Vail shot a glance at the banjo clock on one wall to grudgingly ask, "What happened? Her husband come home unexpected?"

Longarm calmly sat down in the one guest chair provided on his side of the cluttered desk to mildy reply, "I try to avoid married women. Do you have something for me to do around here or would you rather hear the latest news about my bowel movements?"

Vail rummaged through the papers on his desk as he said, "Stick around. We ought to be getting word from the house of detention any time, now. Despite what he likes to be called, Solitaire Stryker is as much a banana as most of his breed."

Longarm didn't have to ask what Billy Vail meant, but the older lawman still explained, "He's yellow and he feels more comfortable hanging in a bunch. I asked you to take him alive if you could and I'm pleased as punch you did. For your favorite uncle is working with the Texas Rangers on this case and I wouldn't be surprised if you get to backtrack that gun for hire all the way down to Brownsville!"

Longarm scowled through the blue haze between them to demure, "I sure hope we ain't thinking about the same Brownsville, in high summer!"

But Vail just smiled and answered, "Brownsville, Texas, where the Rio Grande meets the Gulf of Mexico north of Matamoros."

To which Longarm could only reply, "Aw, shit, had I known that was why you wanted the son of a bitch alive I'd have shot it out with him!"

Chapter 2

"How did you figure he was going to crack so soon?" asked Longarm as the two of them headed down the marble stairwell in answer to the note from the house of detention.

"Paperwork," Vail replied. "I know you young squirts hate paperwork and consider me and Henry fuddy-duddies for shuffling yellow sheets when we could be out sniffing horse turds with the rest of you hard-riding cusses. But the heathen Chinee got it right when they allowed this world was made up of Chinks and Yanks!"

As Longarm held a bronze side door open for his boss on the floor below he dryly remarked, "I suspect you might mean Yin and Yang. I read some and this waitress I know at the Golden Dragon was explaining such notions to me one evening."

As they stepped out into the brighter sunlight to head down the outside steps, Vail replied as dryly, "I'd have been more shocked to find you going sixty-nine with a China doll at high noon."

Longarm said, "That ain't what that Yin and Yang symbol is supposed to stand for, even if it does look sorta like six and a nine of two different colors nestled intimate. The black Yin with a dot of white in it stands for darkness, wetness, earth and womanly ways. The white Yang with a black dot stands for lightness, dryness, heat and manly ways. Each has a dab of the other because the Chinee *Tao* or way of the world holds that nothing can be pure anything. The most dainty young gal might throw a manly punch if she has to and there ain't no man too rough and tough to have a soft spot for something."

At the foot of the steps Vail silently hailed them a hansom with a full fist of cigar as he replied, "Whatever. I was only trying to say what time it was, not build a clock. My point was that it takes all kinds of tracking to catch the sons of bitches. On the surface, our Solitaire Stryker is a hard-cased loner, fast on the draw with nerves of steel."

As the two-wheeled hansom reined in at the high sandstone curb he held his peace. But once they were seated behind the one horse and Vail had given directions to the driver perched above the napes of their necks, Longarm said, "I can't say how fast on the draw he might have been last night. But when he offered he sounded sincere."

Vail sniffed, "Like I said. Surface gloss. Polished head to toe with laudanum and hashish. Real hashish, not that homegrown Mary Jane the Mexicans smoke. The old-time assassins got their handle from the serious hashish they used. They dubbed Stryker *Solitaire* in the first place because he kept to hisself and refused to share the nerve tonics he was getting from home until the prison surgeon found out about it. Once he was in some real solitude, with nothing soothing to drink or smoke, they had to put him in a straitjacket to keep him from beating his own brains out against the wall, see?"

Longarm whistled and allowed he was commencing to. One of the reasons the West, and for that matter the Vic-

11

torian East could get so wild was that, try as they might, the reformers had never managed to outlaw such calming influences as 200 Proof "Trade Whiskey" composed of raw alcohol, caramel coloring and gunpowder for a convincing aftertaste, or Laudanum, a mixture of alcohol and opium, with doctors prescribing opium-based teething lotions for babies whilst suggesting cocaine pills might help a hopeless drunk whup Demon Rum.

Some doctors warned against such practices and a paid-up Mormon was supposed to lay off booze, coffee, tea and tobacco. But despite all the thundering from the sky pilots and W.C.T.U. there was hardly anything a man couldn't buy for his nerves if he had the money. Albeit exotic notions such as Arabian hashish and Mex peyote could be hard to come by when you didn't know the right druggist.

As their hired hack sped them over the cobbles of downtown Denver Longarm mused aloud, "I never got much out of Mary Jane, or marijuana, the few times I've had to be sport at such a gathering. But I did read, somewheres, how that Old Man of the Mountain used to stir his Moslem assassins to superhuman fortitude with refined hashish. I read a man's brain speeds up on the stuff to where time and space all around him seems to slow down. Old-time assassins moved so fast they scared the shit out of regular A'rab swordsmen and a gunslick on the stuff could likely draw a tad faster than natural. That ain't saying he'd *shoot* any better, once he had, of course."

Billy Vail shrugged and asked, "How accurate do you have to aim in your average saloon fight at point-blank range? Like I said, I've been over Stryker's yellow sheets. For a nominal fee he'll pick a fight with the victim of your choice and, nine times out of ten, get away with claiming self-defense because, of course, the gents he's

12

been paid to assassinate during his short career were known gunfighters his clients didn't want to fight themselves."

The distance would have made a serious walk, but it was only a short ride. As they reined in out front of the house of detention Vail hauled out the fare, adding, "The one tenth he can't claim as self-defense were mostly lawmen and this one banker who'd riled customers of our wayward youth, inside. Texas wants him or, better yet, his Texas client, for that banker he gunned in Brownsville. Your favorite uncle is more interested in Stryker's . . . agent, I reckon you'd call the person or persons who set such deals up."

As he reached up to pay their driver Longarm got out on his own side. He didn't need further explanations. But as they headed inside his boss still told him, "You don't just walk up to a rough-looking hairpin in some saloon and ask if he'd care to shoot somebody for you. One of the reasons it's so hard to convict such sons of bitches is that they have their lawyers demand some *motive* for their client shooting a totally strange drunk in a saloon fight."

Longarm quietly suggested, "I've been there, Boss. Pick a noisy payday night to pick a fight in a crowded saloon and it's tough to find any two witnesses who'll agree on just what happened."

"That Brownsville banker was unarmed, and gunned cold sober on a steamboat landing," said the older lawman, adding, "You don't get to claim self-defense when you shoot the town law or a federal deputy on duty. They have the right to shoot *you*, if they ask you to come along quiet and you refuse their first offer."

Longarm grimaced and said, "I noticed that last night in the Silverheels across the creek. Are you suggesting similar conversations have led to grimmer results in other parts?"

Vail snorted, "I told you when I sent you after him that he'd drawn on other lawmen, and won. Let's see how he feels about that now that he's had time to come down from his Seventh Heaven. You see, when the Old Man of the Mountain recruited these young A-rabs to be assassins he told them—"

"I read about the Seven Heavens of Araby," Longarm cut in, trying not to sound so know-it-all as he added, "I read how the Seventh or top level of the hereafter was reserved for martyrs who died, heroic, in some holy cause, such as assassinating somebody the Old Man of the Mountain was pissed off at. Let's ask him where he spent the night, and how he feels about it, now."

Solitiare Stryker wasn't feeling well about anything at all, that morning. They could hear him pissing and moaning from his cell long before they got back to it.

The federal turnkeys had taken the prisoner's belt, kerchief and most everything else but his shirt, socks and the pants he'd pissed in as he lay curled on his side like a whupped hound caught pissing on the rug. But when he sensed the two lawmen staring in at him through the bars of his all-steel patent cell Solitiare leapt up to join them there, pleading, "Listen, you got to get me my medicine. Just one shot from that flask in my saddle bag is all I ask!"

Vail told him, not unkindly, "Your saddle, along with your pony, were impounded last night after you left 'em out front of that saloon. What have you got for me if I send for some . . . medication?"

Stryker showed what the Taoists meant about the blackest Yin having at least a dot of white Yang in it when he shrugged fatalistic and replied, "You already got all I have to offer you and your dad-blasted hangman. I've been expecting your invite to the rope dance for a

14

spell. Like I said last night. I'd rather end as a man with my feet on the ground and a gun in my hand, but since Longarm, there, fights so dirty, I'm ready to face your music without no fuss, if only you'll give me something for my nerves!"

Longarm hadn't seen what Billy Vail had done with his usual stinky cigar. But he saw Vail had gotten rid of it when the older lawman broke out a sort of straw-colored smoke, gripped it betwixt his teeth, and thumb-nailed a matchhead to light up.

Nothing could have smelled worse then Billy Vail's usual brand, but the cell block commenced to reek of the burnt-rope odor of hashish and Stryker only had to sniff it once before he pleaded for just one drag on Billy Vail's funny cigarillo.

The marshal blew a teasing smoke ring through the bars at him and said, "We're still discussing prices. As you just pointed out, you've got to hang no matter what. I'm offering a federal trial and hanging here in Colorado, with enough . . . medication to steady your nerves as you mount them thirteen steps out back and end as a man. My price is the name of the assassination contractor you'd been riding for out of Brownsville."

The doome killer protested, "What sort of a shit would turn in a pal for so little?"

Vail blew more hashish fumes through the bars at him as he calmly replied, "You'd know better than me what it would be worth to you to go to the gallows with a gallant smile instead of shit in your pants. The state of Texas wants to hang you, public, in the courthouse square down Brownsville way, to set an example for other wayward youth. They might or might not offer you some red-eye with your last meal. You ain't about to get anything stronger without offering them some names, and in that case your Texas pals are more likely to find out

15

you turned them in. So you were saying . . . ?"

Stryker shrugged in resignation and murmured, "One. I'll give you a false-hearted woman who steered me wrong about that fucking banker. She assured me the job would go smooth as silk because nobody knew my face along the riverside quay and it would only take split seconds for me to duck out her back door, circle around to nail him as he came back from a business meet in Matamoros and stepped off the steam ferry within the quarter hour!"

Vail said, "The rangers wrote how high water on the Rio Grande fucked things up. You should have called it off for the day when you saw the ferry would be crossing from Old Mexico an hour late. Too many of the regulars recalled your strange face and tense expression when you killed so much time in that riverside cantina. How come you didn't just go on back to . . . this *gal's* back door, you said?"

Stryker hesitated, tried and failed to get something out of the thin haze of hashish by inhaling deep, and replied in a defeated tone, "You want a two-face Creole widow woman they call Madame Belle Lasalle. Runs a boardinghouse handy to the border crossing, upstream and downwind of the more quality quarters of Brownsville."

Vail said, "Keep going. You're doing fine."

So the hired gun explained, "Knock-around riders such as myself don't cotton to signing hotel registers and Madame Lasalle's Creole serving wenches serve you anything you want in bed, from onion soup to a French lesson. So her place is popular with us riders of the Owlhoot Train and, seeing she has our confidence, she's in position to set things up for more prissy folk who'd as soon not do their own fighting, or be in town when a rich uncle cashed in his chips to leave them some."

"Who paid you to have that one banker killed, cold-

16

blooded without a pocket pistol to his name?" asked Vail, trying not to sneer.

Stryker seemed unashamed as he shook his head and said, "Nobody paid me, direct. They made the deal with Madame Lasalle. We never met. Nobody ever told me why the fat old basser had to die. I suspect Madame Belle works that way with conversations such as this one in mind. So I'd never be able to sell you her client's name or reasons. But, what the hell, I might not be in this fix if she hadn't steered me wrong about the ferry from Old Mexico. So she's yours with my blessings and when do I get my nerve medicine?"

Vail passed the lit cigarillo through the bars and broke out five more as the edgy desperado inhaled deeply with his hands cupped around the pungent cigarillo.

Vail said, "I'm a man of my word. You get half a dozen of those a day through your trial and up to the date the judge sets for your last dance out back. If you think of any more names, get word to me by way of the turnkeys and I'll discuss liquid refreshments with you."

Then he nudged Longarm to growl in a more urgent tone, "Let's get out of here. I'm suddenly hungry as a bitch wolf and I know a place over on Larimer as serves truly hot tamales!"

As they strode on out Vail added, "I'll be switched with snakes if I see why. I just had a heroic breakfast and, great day in the morning, I never noticed what a pretty shade brick red was, before. I wonder how it feels when you *inhale* that A-rab shit!"

As they left the building Longarm suggested, "You might have inhaled more than you thought, no offense. Do you really mean to send me all the blamed way to the Gulf of Mexico on the unsupported words of a fucking dope fiend? How do you know he didn't just name this Madame Belle out of pure spite, or thin air? Even if

17

she's really running that boardinghouse by the river I fail to see how we'll ever prove she's any more than a local landlady, whether she's anything more or not!"

Vail led the way on his shorter legs, looking famished, as he told his senior deputy, "You're right. If she's white enough to matter and has a lawyer worth his salt you'd never be able to hold her more than seventy-two hours on the unsupported word of a known criminal. We need us some solid evidence to back up any arrests we make down yonder!"

Longarm said, "Slow down. Folk are commencing to stare at us and you just spooked that dray horse tethered to that post back yonder. If Stryker named this Madame Belle out of pure spite, there might not be a lick of evidence against her for us to worry about!"

Vail agreed, "It's better than fifty-fifty he just fingered someone innocent in Brownsville because he knew we'd check any names he gave us and recalled a Creole gal who'd overcharged him, or said no. But to offer us *any* name from that part of Brownsville, he had to give away the part of Brownsville he's familiar with. So here's what I want you to do, you sneaky young cuss . . ."

Chapter 3

Everybody who'd ever met a Texican had heard Texas was the biggest state in the union. But you had to cross it some by rail to grasp just how big a big they were bragging about.

The distance betwixt the Texas Panhandle and the mouth of the Rio Grande to the southeast was greater than the distance betwixt Chicago and the city of New York. And you had to cross four hundred miles of prairie down from Denver before you ever saw the wide open spaces of the Texas Panhandle.

After that it got worse. Thanks to choosing the wrong side during the War betwixt the States, Texas had been left behind during the postwar railroad construction boom and that, rather than some romantic urge to herd cows many a mile for a good many months, accounted for many a Wild West scene in Ned Buntline's dime novels. But since President Hayes had ended the Reconstruction of the former Confederate states the one called Texas had been catching up and there were fewer summer-long trail drives north every year, as civilization and the Iron Horse inch-wormed in across all that open range.

There was still too much of it for the rails to tie together handy, yet. So you couldn't beeline by rail from Denver to Brownsville and that made for even more pain-in-the-ass days aboard soot grimed-trains that had to huff and puff across summer-browned plains in high summer with all their windows wide open.

Billy Vail's devious plans called for Longarm to travel as often as possible in private compartments, lest anyone getting off in Texas say they'd seen him coming from the north instead of down the border from the west. Time in a railroad compartment passed a whole lot faster in the company of some pretty fellow traveler. But Stryker had already warned them Madame Belle had more than one ready and willing gal on her payroll and it might have taken more than flowers, books and candy to lure a surely respectable gal into a railroad berth with him. So what the hell, he had plenty of magazines and the trancripts of the soon-to-be-late Solitaire Stryker to read. So he read 'em all, more than once, as the state of Texas outside turned out to be mighty tedious to look at as well as bodacious in extent.

The first thing you noticed about Solitaire Stryker's yellow sheets was that his real first name was Wilberforce. Longarm had to agree Solitaire sounded no sillier. After that, Stryker had been born to poor but honest parents on the Brazos, where things might have turned out a tad nicer if Stryker's dad hadn't been killed in the war under General Hood, fighting in Tennessee. That had left a ten-year-old boy who'd needed stronger hands on his reins in the care of a still young and pretty momma, who'd left him to shift for his fool self while she was out hunting for a new man. So, naturally, young Wilberforce had gotten in Dutch stealing chickens for fun and profit, run away before his hearing whilst out on modest bail, and gone from bad to worse, killing his first man,

20

a mean drunk, at the age of sixteen in what had seemed a fair fight to that grand jury in Galveston. A growing boy was allowed to defend himself when a bully with forty pounds and a Paterson Colt conversion picked a bar fight with him.

Drifting west to the even wilder border country as a vaguely sinister young man with no visible means of support, Stryker had killed again in Del Rio, with the grand jury returning the same verdict. Albeit that time it had been just Stryker's word, backed by some good old boys he'd been drinking with, that the Mex ranchero he'd had to shoot had been asking for it. A postscript from the nearby ranger station had raised the first eyebow about a teenaged gringo being caught in the act with a rich ranchero's young widow, by a chambermaid in a Mex posada, just outside the ranger's jurisdiction.

After that, it got tedious as Stryker, growing older but not a hell of a lot wiser, worked his deadly way back and forth along the border, most of the time, with an occasional foray as far north as Wyoming on what had likely been special assignments. Stryker only admitting he'd "had to" kill a gent when he had to do so in front of witnesses. Longarm suspected he was paid more than the usual three figures for such chores, since most of the men he'd killed had been the breed you seldom caught riding past dry gulches alone. If there was anything at all to his story about working through a go-between, Madame Belle or somebody like her, somewhere along the border worked pretty good. A heap of dirty deals were made along the border, where one money could change hands in one jurisdiction for goods and services to be delivered or performed in another.

But wouldn't it be safer to arrange an assassination *north* of the border with some dealer in death based *south* of the border? That one banker had been gunned, in front of more witnesses than planned, as he'd gotten off the ferry on the Texas shore. But, on the other hand, he'd had business dealing in Old Mexico and so, mayhaps, the enemy who'd wanted him put out of business could have been Mexican and, yeah, that worked, for that particular killing. Some of the others read less certain.

But he still had a long ways to go before he could even determine what Madame Belle Lasalle looked like. So there was nothing to do but sit there in his shirt-sleeves, smoking a cheroot with an elbow propped on the sooty sill, softly singing the old church song that best applied to such tedious tasks. It went . . .

"Farther along, we'll know more about it.
Farther along, we'll understand why.
Cheer up, my brothers. Walk in the sunshine.
We'll understand it, all bye and bye . . ."

So then it suddenly commenced to rain as only it can rain in west Texas in high summer after a dry spell, and Longarm was soaked from the waist up in sooty water that ran like ink as he crabbed away from the window to shuck his boots, peel off his wet shirt and damp pants, to move back bare-ass to the open window as the rain kept whipping in to slowly but surely cool and clean his sweat- and soot-grimed hide enough to matter.

The gully washer ended as abrupt as it had begun, as such rains tend to in Texas in high summer. But as the sun came back out to clambake the wet, brown prairie and dry the wind-whipped seat and sill, he and the rolling stock were cleaner than they'd been in recent memory.

Longarm lounged bare-ass for a few more miles. Then, seeing he had to transfer yet another tedious time at the junction they were heading for, he hailed his saddle bags down from the overhead rack to change into fresh, dry

22

sailcloth and sun-faded denim. He'd never brought his fussy tweed suit along in the first place, bound for the Gulf of Mexico where nobody but white men bothered with shirts all that much.

Thus it came to pass that when Longarm got off the one train at the junction to board another, an Anglo peering out from a trackside feed loft from under the brim of a Mexican hat, murmured, "That looks like it could be him! Tall, dark drink of water with a mustache and a six-gun riding cross-draw on his left hip!"

His partner, or, rather, the finger man for the one with the scope-sighted Sprinfield .45-70, snorted in dismissal and pointed out. "Look at that roping saddle he's packing, dressed more like a cowboy than a lawman. Everybody old enough to shave regular sports a mustache, unless he's a fucking pimp."

The one itching to shoot insisted, "He wears his hat in a Colorado crush, he wears his sidearm cross-draw and ain't that a Winchester '73 he has lashed to that stock saddle?"

The finger man soothed, "Nine out of ten old hands favor that same Winchester-Colt combination, seeing both are chambered for the same .44-40 rounds. We ain't all as serious about long-range rifle shots as you, pard. As for his six-gun riding cross-draw, how else would anyone but a trick-shot artist pack one? Everybody from Hickok to the James and Younger boys have noticed it's as easy to draw afoot or on horseback with your side arm riding that ways. That old boy packing the wrong saddle in threadbare jeans you can see he's been wearing a spell ain't that one they call Longarm. He's just another tall, dark rider cut from a pattern that ain't all that rare here in Texas, you know."

"What if I just shoot him for luck?" asked the one with the rifle, adding, "It won't hurt anybody if he's just some

23

saddle tramp and think how pleased the boss will be if we discover I've nailed the one and original Longarm!"

The older and wider fingerman swore softly and said, "I hope you're as good with that rifle as they say you are. I can't say I admire your brains worth shit. You shoot the wrong man and it can hurt like hell for all concerned! There's no telling what sort of a hornet's nest you'd stir up by gunning a total stranger who could have any number of pals anywhere in Texas. He's passing through here aboard a *train*, you thoughtless cuss! After that the boss is likely to hurt the both of us, considerable, should it transpire we've recruited yet more enemies than we really need! Once you have the State of Texas, the United States of America and Los Estados Unidos de Mejico all after you at once, you don't hardly need any number of pissed-off cattlemen at feud with you, hear?"

The one training his sights on Longarm all the while muttered, "Aw, shit, he's boarding that other train and what if we find out he really was the lawman we were posted here to stop?"

The fingerman shrugged and said, "It's better to be safe than sorry. We'll wait out that next train due this afternoon from the north. If nobody looking more like our target gets off, here, we'll wire the boss about that cuss who just passed through. It ain't as if the train he's boarding will make Brownsville within the hour. He's got many a mile and another transfer ahead of him after dark. That'll give our pals in Brownsville all night to set up. When he gets off there, in the gray light of dawn, they can have somebody on the platform for a close-up gander. If he's just an old cowhand they'll let him slide on through and nobody will ever be the wiser. If it looks like a Longarm, walks like a Longarm and quacks like a Longarm they can pluck his feathers then and there, before he can get out of the depot, see?"

24

"Some kids have all the fun," grumbled the rifleman, hauling the muzzle of his Springfield back inside. He started to light a smoke. He didn't strike the match. He found it tedious to be told he had a heap to learn and anybody could see a feed loft was no place to smoke cigars.

The recent rain hadn't gotten at the dusty dry burlap bags filled with parched cracked-corn and mummy-dry oats they were sprawled atop of. So the rifleman contented himself with just sucking on his unlit smoke as the two of them watched that train Longarm had boarded steam off to the southeast, whilst the one he'd gotten down from continued due south. The rifleman asked if they had time to go down the ladder for some coffee and grub before they had to worry about that other train due in from the north.

His older partner said, "We got the time. Time ain't the problem. Having folk here in Parsons Junction remember our strange faces is the problem. So we just stay put, up here where nobody can see us, until that other train shows up, hear?"

The rifleman pouted, "I'm hungry, and dying for a smoke. How long might it take that second infernal train?"

A voice from the gloom further back in the feed loft informed him in a conversational tone that made his blood run cold, "It won't get here before five-fifteen. But railroad timetables are the least of your worries at the moment, you murderous son of a bitch!"

As the both of them whirled to face the dimly visible outline of a lawman who'd found it just as easy to get off the far side of that train as the one facing them, Longarm warned, "Easy with them hands, now. I want you in the Mex sombrero to follow your hands up first. I'll tell

25

you in the gray Stetson when I want you to move one fucking hair!"

"I told you it was him!" sobbed the younger rifleman wearing the Mex hat as he rose unsteadily with his hands held shoulder high. The older, wiser, but now more desperate one didn't answer. Hoping Longarm would be more interested for the moment in his kid sidekick, he went for his shoulder-holstered Starr .38-30.

The kid in the Mex outfit screamed like a gal who'd seen a mouse as Longarm's six-gun roared and the fingerman lost his Stetson and a good part of his skull when all that hot lead exploded his soft wet brains behind the little blue hole in his forehead.

Throwing down on the kid with the smoking muzzle, Longarm snapped, "That wasn't funny. Let's be serious, here. That first shot will earn us some company any minute and I like to get things settled in my own head in simple man-to-man conversations. Who sent you boys to lay for me this far out of Brownsville, Madame Belle Lasalle or some other bad girl from them parts?"

The kid in the Mex outfit replied in as conversational a tone, "I don't know who you're talking about. You spotted the muzzle of that rifle in the sunlight as you were moving along yonder platform, right?"

Longarm said, "Never mind how I spotted you. Suffice it to say I did and we're talking about how come the two of you were up here laying for me, damn your eyes!"

Another voice from some lower depths called out, "This here would be Sergeant Roger Woodward of the Texas Rangers and I'll be coming up this ladder, now. If you blow my head off I'll never speak to you again and you'll never get out of that fucking feed loft alive, hear?"

Longarm turned his head just enough to call back, "Welcome aboard and I'd be the law, too. Deputy U.S. Marshal Custis Long of the Denver District Court."

The scared kid in the Mex outfit mistook Longarm's apparant distraction for a desperate chance. So he took it, and this time Longarm's round of .44-40 nailed him over the heart at point-blank range, setting his frilly fake silk shirtfront aflame as his dead hand fired a still holstered .45 down the side of his bell-bottom pants into a dry bag of oats.

So things were starting to heat up as Ranger Sergeant Woodward poked his head and a Colt Peacemaker up through the ladder trap to order the only man he saw on his feet to just drop that fucking six-gun and grab some fucking air.

Longarm did as he was told; he was no fool. But as he stood there amid the swirling gun smoke and worse he called out, "This is a hell of a time for formalities, Sarge! I'm on your side and this dry feed loft seems to be on fire! Let me show you my badge and then help me haul these bodies out of here. For I doubt your fire volunteers will arrive soon enough to do much good!"

But the ranger insisted, "You just stay put whilst I climb on up for a better look at you, stranger. Anyone can *say* he's the famous Longarm. You're going to have to convince me some."

Longarm protested, "*Later*, for Pete's sake! Can't you see this whole damn building is fixing to go up in flames, with all four of us?"

The ranger calmly replied, "Don't get your shit hot. First we'll find out who the hell you really are, then we'll talk about less important problems, hear?"

Chapter 4

Texas Rangers were supposed to act like that. It could get a man killed, but new recruits were shown clippings of that old newspaper account where the worried mayor of a West Texas town sends for the rangers to put down a riot and, once the train arrives and only one man gets off, they naturally ask how come they only sent one ranger.

The answer the rangers gloried in was, "Why do you need more than one ranger? You only got one riot, right?"

But by the time he'd convinced Sergeant Woodward of his own identity the flames were roaring on all sides, the heat was intense and they barely made it out, themselves, leaving the two dead outlaws for the fire volunteers to worry about.

The part-time firemen of Parsons Junction were a cut above most such small-town outfits. They had their own hand-drawn but steam-powered pump engine and had the fire under control in time to save all but that top floor as Longarm and the ranger watched from across the way.

By this time Longarm had brought Sergeant Woodward up to date on the little he really knew about the ambush there at the junction. Woodward agreed the gang Solitaire Stryker rode with had likely put two and two together as soon as they'd heard Stryker had been taken alive by such a well-known lawman. It would have hardly taken a college professor to surmise that a pal running on laudanum and hashish would sell them out for certain. Woodward opined, "It was still dumb for them to try and stop you here, when they still had time to split up and run for it, down yonder."

Longarm shrugged and said, "They might have hoped to save themselves some heavy lifting. Styker was likely lying. But if his Madame Belle really owns real estate down Brownsville way, she might have thought it would cost less to have me killed than it would to liquidate her boardinghouse property in the time it would take me to get there alive."

A young squirt in a seersucker jacket and straw hat seemed to know Sergeant Woodward as he crossed over from the pumping crew to join them near the railroad fence line, saying, "The firemen tell me they just found two dead bodies, or what was left of the same, up in that burnt-out feed loft! Might you be able to enlighten our readers about that, Sergeant Woodward?"

The ranger explained to Longarm, "This would be reporter Breslin from the *Parsons Junction Journal* ah, what did you say your name was, deputy?"

Longarm calmly replied, "Smiley. Riding out of Denver for Uncle Sam with the late Deputy Custis Long. He'd be the taller of the two toasted cadavers across the way. Place caught on fire when we shot it out with two outlaws who fired on us first. Lord knows why. My poor sidekick, we called him Longarm, went down along with one of the outlaws in the point-blank gunplay. The other got away, dad blast his murdersome hide."

Sergeant Woodward just stood there owl-eyed as the reporter gasped, "Great day in the morning! The famous gunfighter, Longarm, has met his fate here in Parsons Junction? Jesus H. Christ! I got to run this in banner type and put it out on the wire! For this is going to make our town as famous as Deadwood or Dodge!"

As he scampered off, the ranger dryly remarked, "I follow your drift. But we're going to have to clear it with my captain and, even if he allows you to stay dead, won't the crooks wonder when that one who got away, according to you, never comes back?"

Longarm asked, "Why in thunder would any gunslick who'd just lived through a desperate gunfight head back to his usual haunts, leaving a dead lawman and a dead pal someone might identify behind him?"

Woodward grinned like a mean little kid and said, "Hot damn! You're as good as they say you are, Longarm! Let's go tell the captain how you mean to pussyfoot on down to Brownsville with them crooks slapping one another on the back because they've kilt you!"

Longarm said he had to pick up the saddle and possibles he'd dropped in the weeds on the far side of the tracks, lest some other wicked children be tempted. Woodward said he'd go fetch an extra pony from the livery where he'd left his own saddled bronc. So they parted friendly for the moment and met up again a few minutes later to ride out to the ranger station on the edge of town.

The Texas Rangers had been organized in the beginning to fight the Indians, mostly Comanche and Kiowa Apache, as irregular cavalry for the Republic of Texas. As they'd evolved into more of a police force, replacing the hated state police of the recent Reconstruction, they'd become their own peculiar institution. Organized along military lines like the Canadian Mounties, their only of-

30

ficial uniform was a small silver badge. They favored dark suits in cool weather, wore white shirts with dark pants and no vests in hot weather, and *told* folks what their ranks might be. Sergeant Woodward felt no call to wear stripes on his sleeve and when they got over to his company headquarters building, out front of a pole corral, his boss, a Captain Yokem, wore no other indications of rank than his own ranger badge on clean white cotton.

Captain Yokem was friendly enough, but didn't much approve of the way Damnyankee federal lawmen coddled prisoners.

As the three of them shared some bourbon and branch water from the file cabinet in Yokem's office, the graying whipcord and whalebone older lawman complained, "By right that Texican killer you're holding up Denver way ought to be ours to hang, and you can rest assured the State of Texas would never cater to his unnatural appetites for narcotics!"

Longarm regarded his highball fondly as he softly asked, "What sort of narcotic are we talking about, alcohol, caffeine, nicotine or that hashish he's so fond of? None of 'em are supposed to be good for you, but under current legislation you can even send a prisoner in jail a devil's food cake as long as you don't bake no saws into it."

Yokem said, "You know what I'm talking about. Offering a prisoner dope to get him to talk is the same as beating the information out of him, if you ask me!"

Longarm shrugged and said, "I suspect Solitaire Stryker found old Billy's methods less painsome. I asked Billy if we might not be sort of questioning a prisoner unconstitutional. He assured me *quid pro quo*, or something for something, was a long-established legal principle, and how would we have gotten toad squat out of a man on his way to the gallows with no call to like us at all? We're dealing with one or more assassination contractors down along the border, Captain. Stryker ain't the only killer riding for them. I just killed two more of the gang this very day!"

Yokem grudgingly conceded, "I never said we had to give them any breaks, damn it. But you Denver boys are surely cutting it close to the bone, what with pushing dope to dope fiends and asking us to lie to the county coroner about them bodies from that burnt-out feed loft!"

Longarm soothed, "Nobody's asking anybody around here to lie, Captain. Your sergeant, here, was listening when it was *me* who told that reporter I'd been killed and burnt beyond recognition this afternoon. Neither you nor any of your rangers witnessed exactly what happened up yonder as the place first caught on fire. So all I'm asking either of you to do is *nothing*! If you just ain't ready to comment, pending way more investigation, that ought to give me time to catch another train to a border town upstream from Brownsville and just drift in by riverboat like the footloose cuss I've always been."

Yokem laughed in spite of himself and declared, "You got more balls than your average pool hall. But, if we do go alone with your harebrained notions, how will we ever find out who those jaspers up in that feed loft really were?"

Longarm shrugged and said, "There's one way to find out. I can always ask their friends, once I catch up with 'em. Getting on down to Brownsville the long way 'round ought to give news of today's gunfight and fire time to get there first. It's the simple truth that as things now stand neither of those bodies can be identified for certain. If you let it stand that one of 'em's said to be the lawman they were laying for, here in Parsons Junction, they shouldn't be expecting or suspecting me when I finally show up."

Sergeant Woodward asked, "What if they don't? Do you expect any crook with a lick of sense to offer a total stranger more than the correct time of day if he should ask?"

Longarm soberly replied, "Not hardly. I got to see if I can convince them I ain't such a total stranger."

Captain Yokem asked, "How? You don't even know who *they* are!"

Longarm smiled wryly and replied, "I got one name and address. Whether Stryker was dealing from the top or the bottom of the deck I got to stay somewhere in Brownsville and it may as well be that transient boardinghouse near the scene of that banker's murder. But now, if it's all the same to you gents, I got some chores to tend before that five-fifteen southbound. Do we have us a deal?"

The ranger captain grudginly conceded, "I can't lie flat-out to my own superiors, if they challenge reporter Breslin's thrilling account of your demise. But I have no call to volunteer any information, unless, that is, they decide to give the famous Longarm a swell funeral at the expense of our own taxpayers!"

Longarm soothed, "That's one of the chores I have to tend. I aim to see my body's shipped back to Denver, along with that of my prisoner. The one I kilt so gallant, going down. I'll be wiring my home office as Deputy Smiley, who's for real, and another tall dark drink of water should anyone in Brownsville ask their pals in Denver."

"How do you know they have pals in Denver?" asked Yokem.

Longarm said, "Their known associate and subcontractor, Solitaire Stryker, must have been in Denver on some chore for them. His yellow sheets have it that as a rule he lurks close as he can to border crossings. After

33

that, Marshal Vail ordered me out in the field undercover. But they had those dry gulchers waiting here where they knew I'd have to change trains within easy rifle range of that feed loft. Add it up."

So they did, they shook on it, and parted friendly. The sergeant rode Longarm back to the center of town and once they had the riding stock in the livery, with Longarm's stock saddle and possibles safely stored in their tack room, they split up to get cracking at their different but complimentary chores.

Longarm went first to the Western Union near the railroad stop to send two wires to different people at the same street address without naming the Denver Federal Building. He told the clerk behind the counter he was paying for the first one personal and wanted it delivered at least half an hour ahead of the other. Western Union didn't advertise them. But they had many a mile of wire strung across many a mile of federal open range, military and Indian reserves. So one hand washed the other and he was counting on them giving that one a low priority, to be sent when the lines weren's busy with profitable public traffic.

His personal message, sent to Uncle Henry in care of their office number, read, WAYWARD CHILD NOT AS NAUGHTY AS YOU MAY HAVE HEARD STOP SHE IS SORRY IF SHE WORRIED YOU STOP SHE PROMISES TO BEHAVE AS YOU TOLD HER NOW STOP COUSIN CRAWFORD

He knew old Henry knew he often used Crawford as an alias because he was proud of the Doctor Crawford Long who'd invented painless surgery just in time for the war back East and because Reporter Crawford of the *Denver Post* was a pest who kept printing big fibs about him. So once their clerk-typist figured out who'd sent such a loco message he'd be able to decode it easy enough.

The second message read, more soberly, DEPUTY LONG KILLED BY PERSON OR PERSONS UNKNOWN STOP SENDING HIS BODY AND THAT OF ONE HE TOOK WITH FOR YOUR EDIFICATION STOP DETAILS WHEN I RETURN STOP INTEND TO DO SO AS SOON AS I WRAP UP HERE STOP DEPUTY SMILEY

He addressed that one directly to Marshal Vail, knowing old Billy would share the joke with the real Smiley and tell him what to say when and if anybody asked.

The rangers had told him the bodies would be in the town morgue. Or the basement of their druggist-coroner, if you wanted to be picky. Sergeant Woodward met him there after Longarm had arranged with the railroad dispatcher to deliver the toasted bodies, suitably boxed on beds of rock salt and cracked ice.

Regarding the blackened remains in the earth-floored celler under that drugstore, with Sergeant Woodward and the fat cheerful druggist cum coroner, Longarm wondered if the salt and ice would be needed. Mummies in the Colorado State Museum on 14th Avenue didn't look anymore dried out and crispy. When he asked, the druggist cum coroner suggested the rock salt, alone, would do them as far as Denver.

Sergeant Woodward said, "I just had a talk with the old Dutchman who used to have that feed loft. I told him if he expects to file insurance claims he won't want us indicting him on aiding and abetting. So he's seen the light and agreed to quit aiding and abetting. He admitted they slipped him two dollars for the private use of his feed loft for the day. When they told him they didn't want to be disturbed up yonder he took them for a couple of queers who wanted to spend some time alone. They could have hired a hotel room for less. But sodomy's a jailable offense in Texas and hotel clerks tend to worry about that."

Longarm asked, "Did they offer the loft owner any names?"

The ranger nodded and said, "He says they called one another Red and Spike. The shorter one used to have red hair. The taller one you identified as that Deputy Long would have had dark hair and a mustache if they hadn't gone up in smoke. The one who . . . got away must have been Spike. He describes as about forty, going gray at the temples with a hare lip he tries in vain to hide under his own mustache."

Longarm nodded and said, "I'll ask about him along my merry way. I doubt either name appears on any birth certificate. But like the old song says, farther along, we'll know more about it."

So the coroner, who served as the local undertaker when he wasn't selling pills upstairs, allowed he'd see to it that both bodies were sent to Denver, with his services charged to Uncle Sam, and Woodward helped Longarm get himself and his baggage aboard the five-fifteen as soon as it got in.

Then things got tedious again and as the sun went down to the west Longarm stared morosely out at the flat expanses of low chaparral and Spanish bayonet, hoping he knew what he was doing and facing another night alone on the move to worry about it.

Chapter 5

Shallow draft paddlewheelers could navigate the Rio Grande further upstream than Del Rio, but didn't bother. Del Rio was the official head of navigation, better than three hundred miles northwest of the gulf, because nobody much had settled the Big Bend country further up and the river was too swift and sandy by the time you got past the mouth of the Pecos beyond the Big Bend.

Longarm wasn't about to travel any three hundred miles by steamboat if it could be avoided. He avoided it easily by getting off another train the next morning at Laredo, a hard day's run upstream and an easier one downstream to Brownsville. He'd chosen to steamboat that far because that was where the rail line he was riding met up with the Rio Grande and because Laredo was a big enough town for a stranger to sashay about in without everybody rushing to their front windows as he passed.

At the steamboat landing he discovered he had time for another wire to the home office and another chore he'd been studying on aboard the train. He went first to the Western Union and, addressing this one to Billy Vail's private residence on Sherman Street, sent, HAVING

WONDERFUL TIME WISH YOU WERE HERE STOP YOUR LOVING NEPHEW

Then he scouted up a print shop with the longer missive he'd composed aboard the train with more thought.

When he allowed he only needed a dozen or so copies the old-timer running the shop from under a green eyeshade allowed they could stick the type and run a dozen copies on their proof press for five dollars. So Longarm told him to go ahead and went next door for a bowl of chili whilst the old-timer "stuck" or set the type and ran off the dozen reward posters on his proof press, which was really a fancy name for a heavy roller, running on rails to either side of the face-up type. To "pull a proof" you inked the type, gently placed a sheet of paper on the same, and ran the roller over the back of the sheet to press the other side firmly down against the inked type.

Then, if you knew what you were doing, you could lift the paper off without smudging it and set aside your printed proof to dry. It didn't take the old-timer as long to fill Longarm's order as it took Longarm to fill his gut with chili con carne and tuna pie. The tuna pie they served along the border was made from tuna cactus fruit, not fish.

As they settled up the old-timer asked Longarm, "Might you be a bounty hunter, old son?"

When Longarm said that was close enough, the job printer nodded and said, "Thought so. This Morman Mike Mason you'd be offering a hundred dollars for sounds mean, for a man with a hundred-dollar bounty. How much is he really worth to you, once somebody turns him in to you at . . . Del Rio?"

Longarm had long since learned how smart it was to allow others to feel they were outsmarting you. So he smiled sheepishly and confessed, "All right, a man in my business is entitled to an honest profit and so mayhaps

38

Mormon Mike is worth five hundred over to New Mexico Territory. But keep it quiet and if it's all the same to you I got me a steamboat to catch."

The Laredo resident said the only steamboat due before noon would be running down the river, not back up it to Del Rio.

As Longarm rolled up the dozen reward posters he nodded soberly and declared, "If I wanted to spend the day in Del Rio I'd have never left my office there, would I?"

So he got no further argument and in no time at all he'd boarded a sternwheeler bound for the gulf, stored his saddle and possibles in a small but private cabin handy to the shithouse over the paddlewheel and headed foreward to catch such breeze as there might be as the Texas sun tried hard to evaporate the muddy Rio Grande out from under them.

"My land, it's hot!" sighed a shemale voice to his left just as he'd gotten a cheroot going from betwixt cupped hands. Longarm allowed it surely was as he turned to regard his shemale fellow traveler. It was easy. Her face was too freckled and sweaty to be called fashionable, but she was young and pretty too, if you cared for country gals who wore straw blond braids and no corsets under their blue-checked summerweight calico dresses with the bodice cut lower than current fashion dictated. The fashionable young things posing for *The Woman's Home Companion* hadn't been posing under a Texas sun in high summer.

He ticked his hat brim to her and asked if it was all right with her if he went on smoking. He knew better than to offer a lady a smoke of her own in public. Secret vices were more fun shared in private.

She said she didn't mind the smell of his three-for-a-nickel skinny cheroot and allowed she was Lavinia Norris, bound for Brownsville on business. She said her friends all called her Lava.

Longarm didn't ask what her business might be. He said his friends called him Mike, then hesitated just enough for her to wonder before he lamely offered "Mike Carpenter" to sound more formal. A carpenter usually worked alongside a mason, didn't he?

But before he'd finished his cheroot she'd told him, anyway, she was bound for Brownsville in search of a new start after leaving a brute who'd threatened to strike her if she ever brought up the topic of his late hours again.

Longarm had cultivated the art of getting total strangers to confide things they'd have never confessed to closer friends. So he just went on staring on downstream as she told him in a small worried voice how she'd heard a man could bring things home from a house of ill repute. He managed not to show any great interest when she timidly asked him how a girl might know if her wicked man had clapped her up.

Not meeting her eyes, Longarm quietly asked, "The regimental surgeon told us, when I was in an army one time. But I fear what he told us about such matters ain't for delicate ears, Miss Lava."

She said, "Oh, please tell me! I'm so worried and maybe not quite as delicate as you take me for. I know I look young. But I'm over twenty-one and not exactly a . . . maiden pure."

Longarm flicked his smoked down cheroot off to starboard, since she was alongside at port, and explained in a detached and even tone, "It depends a heap on how long it's been since you and the suspect were . . . intimate enough to matter."

She fluttered her lashes and looked away to confide, "I told him he'd never touch me if he went back to that

40

parlor house again, but he did, so I never and that was, let's see, a good three days before I had my last . . . you know."

Longarm did know. He calmly suggested, "It takes nine or ten days for the symptoms of either the clap or the syph to show. Blue balls show up sooner and of course you catch crabs direct."

"Oh, my Lord, there's more than one sort of clap you brutes can give a poor girl?" she moaned.

He dryly suggested, "Few men have ever caught any social disease from another man. But the question before the house is how long has it been since your last period?"

She blushed, covered her face with her hands, and blurted, "A little over a week and you shouldn't use such language!"

He shrugged and said, "You were the one who asked. I don't know how to talk about such matters more delicate. But speaking as an old army man, I'd say you're in pretty good shape for a gal who'd been consorting with a dedicated rake. Figuring three days prior, three to five days during and seven or eight days since your last period, you ought to be out of the woods if you've suffered no symptoms so far."

She asked, "How can I be sure? What are these symptoms you warned me about?"

Longarm heaved a vast sigh and said, "This is getting past clinical into cruelty to dumb animals, Miss Lava. I'm a natural man and you're a good-looking woman. You know what's likely to happen if I offer you an unlicensed medical examination and you take me up on it, don't you?"

She demurely replied, "Do you know what to look for, down there?"

To which he could only reply, "Well, sure I do. Nobody would worry about catching social diseases if noth-

41

ing happened to their privates. But don't you reckon you'd be safer asking a regular doctor to have a peek under your skirts?"

She didn't meet his eyes, but her voice was impish as she asked him, "Safe in what way? I just told you I was hardly a maiden pure and it's been over two weeks since any man has . . . examined me."

So they went to his cabin and he made certain the door was barred as Lava Norris got ready to be "examined."

When he saw she'd stripped to her knee-length socks and positioned herself on his berth with his pillow under her trim young rump and her firm slender thighs spread wide, Longarm sat down beside her to shuck his own duds as he began by parting her straw-colored pubic hairs with his fingers in search of crabs.

He didn't find any. But since her pink clit was peering out of the thatch fully aroused, he proceeded to pet it with his free hand whilst he unbuckled his belt with the other, casually assuring her, "You ain't got crabs or blue balls."

She thrust her pelvis higher, murmuring, "I'm so happy to hear that! Don't stop what you're doing. It feels so nice. Do you think I might be coming down with those other nasty ailments, Mike?"

Longarm grinned wolfishly and declared, "If you have I'm sure likely to catch one or the other. But let's just part those sweet lips some and have us a look."

Dropping the last of his duds on the rug, Longarm knelt on the berth betwixt her widespread knees to open the moist pink gates of Paradise with his hands, observing, "No sign of any syph sores or clap discharge. You sure do keep yourself nice and clean down here, Miss Lava."

She modestly replied, "Thank you. It means a lot to me to look my best for gentleman callers."

So he proceeded to kiss his way up her bare belly as he ran two stiff fingers in and out of her lest she mistake his intent. Her cupcake tits of modest size but heroic firmness distracted him some. So she was moving her hips and begging for it by the time they locked lips and he ran his throbbing organ grinder up into her with a moan of pure pleasure.

It was a caution how men forgot, betwixt times, just how good that felt the first time you shoved it into a total stranger. It only got to be a chore once a gal knew you well enough to start nagging you to spend more time with her and show her some respect by begging for it harder.

But as the rightly described Miss Lava locked her long, slender legs around his waist and tried to swallow his tongue, Longarm reflected on how well the term, "honeymoon" described those first romantic romps in strange surroundings. Some kindly philospher had once remarked, in French, that nine out of ten women were worth screwing, whilst that tenth one made for a nice change of pace. So most any man and woman of any description could enjoy a swell time together for at least a dozen or more times. That was doubtless why there were so many men stuck with ugly wives or scolding shrews after all-too-short honeymoons. That Professor Darwin over to England held that Mother Nature seemed hell-bent on preserving the species with all sorts of tricks.

So despite the heat and humidity the daylong run downstream to the quay at Brownsville passed more pleasantly for the both of them than either might have managed alone. By the time she'd shyly suggested it might feel cooler if she got on top, followed by a sponge bath and a quarter hour's worth of dog style, Longarm was commencing to suspect Miss Lava was a woman of the world indeed and might have made up all that shit about a false-hearted lover who'd left her hard up with a worried mind and a good excuse to take her duds off. But, what the hell, he'd assured her his name was Mike Carpenter and said he hailed from New Mexico Territory. So all seemed fair enough and it sure beat just sweating like so for no good reason.

The day was about done when their steamboat whistle tooted for the last bend north of Brownsville. That was when Lava shyly told him she wanted to get off alone, lest someone on shore take her for the sort of woman who picked up men aboard steamboats.

Longarm didn't argue. He gravely told her he had his own reputation as a virgin to maintain. So they quickly dressed and parted laughing with a thoroughly screwed-out kiss.

Longarm took his own good time and never saw Lava go ashore. He got off with the last passengers, toting his saddle and possibles down the gangplank on his left hip with his .44-40 grips just ahead of the swells and his gun hand free.

But nothing happened as he got safely ashore and headed up the quay toward the ferry landing and that boardinghouse run by Madame Belle Lasalle, if there was any such place or person.

Longarm had worked more than one case around the estuary of the Rio Grande and knew Brownsville of old. There wasn't a hell of a lot of Brownsville to know. Named for an old army outpost from the tense days leading up to the Mexican War back in the forties, Brownsville had a mixed population of less than a thousand households, mostly Mex, with the rest a bewildersome mish-mash from all the other seaports of the world. English-speaking Anglos and French-speaking Creoles ran the town. Creole was a word abused by a lot of folk who claimed to be Creole.

The word had started out Spanish, as *criollo*, a contemptuous term with the same meaning as "House Nigger" in the Old South. But as adopted and spelled by French settlers in the West Indies and Louisiana, *Creole* stood for a French subject of any complexion born in the Western Hemisphere. The Empress Josephine of France had been a Creole, hailing as she had from the French island of Martinique. Nobody had said she hadn't been of pure French blood whilst she'd been Empress of France.

Since her time the term had spread to include most anyone in the West Indies or along the Gulf Shore who didn't want to say they were Anglo or Mex. So farther along, as the song went, he'd find out just what Madame Belle looked like, if she was there at all.

On another part of the quay the innocent-looking young thing who'd told him her name was Lava had been met with a carriage from the parlor house she was bound for. As she drove away with two other whores, one of them asked how her trip down the river had been.

The gal whose real name sounded nothing like Lava smiled like Mona Lisa and said, "Not bad at all. Met a right nice-looking gent aboard the boat with a pecker to go with those broad shoulders."

"How much did you charge him?" asked one of her fellow working girls.

The one who'd just serviced Longarm gratis sighed and confessed, "Nothing. I could tell he wasn't the sort of man who paid for it and, what the hell, they say practice makes perfect."

The older whore sighed and said, "I used to have such romantic feelings when the world was younger. What line of work was this handsome devil in, seeing you doubted he could pay?"

The thoroughly satisfied blonde said, "Oh, I reckon he *could* have paid. I just didn't think he *would* have. He

45

said he hailed from New Mexico Territory, and he was traveling light with a double-action Colt .44 and a repeating rifle. So I guess you know what that adds up to!"

The other whore across from her nodded soberly and said, "I read in the papers about that Lincoln County War. If you ask me, it was sort of dumb of you to mess with a gunfighter on the run!"

Chapter 6

There really was a boardinghouse run by a Madame Belle Lasalle near the ferry crossing. She turned out to be a motherly-built old gal of around fifty with soft olive features and anthracite eyes hard enough to make your average Apache mind his manners.

She let him introduce himself as Mike Carpenter from out New Mexico way, looking to sign on aboard the clippership, *Spanish Dancer* as soon as she got back that way from around the horn. There was such a vessel. It was owned by a Texican lady friend and so he knew for a fact he had a good three weeks before he had to make up any more fibs about signing on.

Madame Belle told him she had one room upstairs that had just been vacated and added it would set him back a dollar a day for the room with board. They both knew he could have stayed in a first-rate hotel and et in restaurants for a little more than that. But he paid up front like a sport to the end of the week and Madame Belle's slight accent got a shade warmer.

She said he'd shown up too late for their regular set-down supper. But she'd have her help rustle him up some

47

soup and sandwiches whilst he stored his gear upstairs. She saved herself the climb by yelling for a pretty little quadroon to show their new guest to that room Mister Gleason had been boarding in.

Longarm didn't say anything as he followed the young gal upstairs through the gloom, admiring her shapely *derrier*, as you called it in Creole French. There was enough lamplight from below to see she was built swell. She likely called herself Creole instead of Colored, seeing she worked for Madame Belle and went by the name of Monique.

As she showed him into a fair corner room that wasn't worth any buck a day despite cross-ventilation behind jalosied windows, allowing air with privacy at the same time, Longarm casually asked if they were talking about the same Gleason he knew from New Mexico, a big husky cuss with bushy black hair.

Monique replied, "*Mais non, Me'sieu.* The one we had staying here was short and not very strong-looking, with how you say, rusty red hair?"

That sounded close enough to the shorter one he'd shot up in Palmers Junction. But he naturally said, "Has to be another Gleason, then. They don't even describe as kin."

Then he tipped her two bits for her trouble as she handed over the key. She thanked him "Beaucoup!" but didn't seem as astounded as your average chambermaid should have for a day's wages in a bunch. So, right, she'd gotten used to serving customers who paid way more than usual for the comforts of home with nobody questioning their sources of income.

After Monique left he took his time draping his borrowed stock saddle over the foot of the bed, hung his hat on a peg, but went back down with his .44-40 still riding his left hip.

Madame Belle's boardinghouse was, as usual, laid out

like the private home it had once been. Most good-sized Anglo family homes of the times were laid out much the same with two or more stories of bedchambers above an almost standard parlor floor plan, with the visitor's parlor and family living room to one side of the central hallway and the dining room to the other, with the kitchen as big or bigger, to the rear. As he came down the stairs he saw they'd fitted out the front parlor to his left like the lobby of a hotel, with a potted fern in the bay window and plenty of cane and wicker easy chairs with coffee tables between, all riding on a woven grass rug. Wool carpeting and upholstry rotted whilst you looked at it, this close to the Gulf of Mexico.

There were two other boarders sharing an ashtray and gossip in a far corner. Longarm nodded to them but sat down closer to the hallway arch, seeing he was expecting to be served some grub. He ran a casual eye over a newspaper someone had left on a table near an empty chair. Since a stranger in from New Mexico Territory would have no call to be too interested in a small-town Texas newspaper Longarm contented himself with reading the headline of the *Parsons Junction Journal* upside down. That reporter Breslin had sure been excited about the death of a famous lawman up their way.

Longarm ignored the hammered copper ashtray handy to his own seat and sat silently. He waited for them to get cracking with the damned soup and sandwiches. One of the other boarders across the way, a gent of around forty in a Panama suit of rumpled white linen cleared his throat and, without rising, called out, "I'd be Tom Corrigan. The greaser, here, answers to Juan Pablo Jones."

The younger, somewhat darker stranger dressed in a light gray charro outfit trimmed in black lace quietly suggested, "My father's people were Welsh, look you. My mother, it's true, was of Spanish extraction and if anyone around here wants to call her a greaser again I fear we may see blood before this night is over, you see."

The one calling himself Corrigan didn't sound scared as he soothed, "Aw, nobody ever mentioned *tu madre, amigo mio*. I was only introducing you to this handsome stranger, here. What did you say your name was, handsome stranger?"

Longarm smiled coldly and replied, "Carpenter. Mike Carpenter. And you do have a dangerous way with words, Mister Corrigan. If you want to fight, just say so. Don't sniff around my ass like a hound dog trying to determine where we stand."

"Oh, where *do* we stand?" asked the man in white linen, thoughtfully.

Longarm shrugged and stared back just as hard as he replied, "Any fucking way you want it, Mister Corrigan. I never came here looking for trouble. But when trouble comes my way I ain't one for backing away from it. Used to be this cowspread cook who liked to bully me when I was younger and less set in my ways. I tried every way I knew how to get along with the contrary shit. As you can likely guess, I had to gun a man who was way too big for me to fistfight in them days. Ain't it a caution how, no matter how nice you are to natural bullies, they can't seem to live and let live?"

Corrigan decided, "Call me Tom, Mike. Madame Belle says you just come down from New Mexico Territory?"

Longarm tried to sound mollified as he replied in a friendlier tone, "Everybody has to come from some direction. I've come from hither and I've come from yon. Where I've been is ancient history and I ain't too certain about where I'm going."

Another serving gal entire came in with a tray of soup

and sandwiches with a mug of coffee. She looked to be part Mex and wasn't as pretty as the dusky Monique. Longarm told her he didn't care for any coffee. She wasn't paid to argue. As she took the coffee back to the kitchen Longarm found the onion soup right tasty and the French bread and soft cheese with canned ham sandwiches were tolerable.

The dusky Monique came in with an expectant expression and a box of cuban cigars, telling Longarm, the after-supper smokes were courtesy of Madame Belle. She didn't look as surprised when Longarm politely told her he didn't smoke, either. Juan Pablo Jones rose gracefully to follow her back to the kitchen, casually allowing he could use a good cigar if it was on the house.

Tom Corrigan rose with a yawn to allow he had to go have a crap. As he passed the table where the newspaper lay, the man in white linen asked in a desperately disinterested voice whether the new man on the premises had heard about that shoot-out up to Parsons Junction.

The lawman who'd been killed there, according to that headline, said he'd never heard of the place and asked who'd shot it out with whom.

Corrigan said, "That famous lawman, Longarm, and two others nobody's identified, so far. The lawman got one. The other killed him and got away. Ain't that a bitch?"

Longarm shrugged and said, "Nobody *I* gave a shit about got killed." And this was the simple truth as soon as you studied on it.

So Corrigan left, Longarm finished his snack and, meeting that Mex maid in the hall, allowed he was headed over to the waterfront to feed the seagulls or whatever.

Then he left, wishing he could be certain nobody was tailing him. But since he couldn't, he had to stroll past

51

many an open-front cantina offering anything from Mexican pulque to Anglo mint juleps, damn them one and all!

Back at the boardinghouse, the Mex gal having reported his evening stroll, Madame Belle was up in Longarm's hired room with Corrigan and Juan Pablo Jones, studying all the possibles they'd spread across the counterpane of Longarm's hired bedstead.

Madame Belle waved one of the reward posters Monique had told her their new boarder had been packing in a saddlebag as she triumphantly decided, "It fits. This poster describes our Mike Carpenter from New Mexico to a tee, once you change his handle to Mormon Mike Mason!"

"He could be a lawman looking for another Mike who sort of favors him," Tom Corrigan pointed out.

There was naturally no *picture* of the wanted Mormon Mike on the poster Longarm had paid for in Laredo. The new Ben Day process allowing one to print halftone photographs was still too new, and expensive, for even Frank and Jesse or The Kid to rate printed likenesses on their reward posters. So all they had to go on was Longarm's modest description of his own face and figure, along with a criminal record of some length and no substance that could be checked for certain.

Juan Pablo Jones mused, "Our mysterious new boarder refuses coffee and tobacco, as Mormons are said to."

Corrigan snorted, "Are you accusing a hairpin who just now offered to fight me of religious purity, Juan Pablo?"

Madame Belle was the one who pointed out, "These posters he seems to have collected say he was raised in Utah Territory in the Mormon faith. They do not accuse him of piety. But tell me, M'sieu Corrigan, do you eat meat on Friday, despite your upbringing, just because you have broken a few less important laws?"

The Irish American chuckled sheepishly and confessed, "As a matter of fact, I have. But it didn't feel right and I follow your drift. So maybe a hired gun could abide by his momma's menu the way Johnny Ringo is said to abstain from pork."

Juan Pablo Jones said, "Aw, Johnny Ringo ain't no infernal Jew, even if his real name's Rhinegold. He could be a plain old Dutchman, you know."

Tom Corrigan said, "Johnny Ringo's religious affiliations ain't the question before the house. We want to know whether Mormon Mike Mason and that Mike Carpenter boarding with us are one and the same!"

Madame Belle said, "*Merde alors*, what does it matter? He says he is hoping to sail away on a clipper ship, as one might expect a man with a price on his head to desire, *hein*? Let us put everything back where we found it before he comes back and regards us as a den of thieves. If he is really this Mormon Mike, so be it. If he is some other Mormon with a desire to amass reward posters, who cares? He is nothing to us or anyone we know in any case, *non*?"

Tom Corrigan said, "*Non*. We've lost Stryker and Gleason. Bunny Weed might or might not come back. That newspaper story says the rangers think Longarm might have winged old Bunny in that wild and wooly shoot-out and, even if he got away clean, he might be well advised to head out Arizona way for his health until things cool down. So any way you slice it, we're getting a tad shorthanded and I sort of *like* that Mormon cuss. Ain't many men as ready and willing to stand up to this child like that. So if only we could be certain he's the Mormon gunfighter described on these fliers and not some other mean Mormon out to collect the bounty on him!"

Madame Belle suggested, "Why don't we find out?

53

There is an address on these posters offering a hundred dollars for no more than a hint, *hein*? Why not wire this species of a private agency in Del Rio and see what *they* have to tell us?"

Juan Pablo Jones protested, "Turn a gentleman of the road in, for a pathetic hundred dollars?"

The hard-eyed motherly landlady laughed dirty and explained, "*Mais non*, nobody said one word about reporting the possible whereabouts of Mormon Mike Mason. My suggestion is that we wire those bounty hunters in Del Rio, reporting we have arrived in Brownsville and await further instructions. Then we sign it Mike Carpenter and wait to regard what sort of answer we recieve."

Juan Pablo Jones laughed and declared, "Spoken like a lady I shall never in this world play poker with! Any instructions at all will mean the rider that goes with this roping saddle is packing these reward posters as a bounty hunter. If he's who we think he might be, the fake name he gives shouldn't mean anything to that . . . let's see, Emerson Private Investigations Agency. So they'll ignore our wire or ask us why on earth we ever wired them."

"I like it." Tom Corrigan decided, chiming in with, "Sending a wire signed Mike Carpenter to this Emerson outfit will settle something else that just now struck me, studying these crisp clean flyers!"

When Juan Pablo asked what that might be, the older man in white linen said, "Where he got 'em. Why he's packing so many of 'em."

Juan Pablo said, "*Ay chihuahua*, it's natural to gather reward posters with one's own name on them. I still have one of the first flyers ever posted on me, down in Vera Cruz."

Tom Corrigan shrugged and said, "Maybe. I'd like to be certain a real bounty-hunting outfit posted flyer-one on a real Mormon Mike! I know more than one job printer here in Brownsville who'd be proud to run you off all the reward posters you could pay for. So let's make certain this Emerson Private Investigations Agency is really there at this address in Del Rio before we worry about whether they really want any Mormon Mike Mason, see?"

He got no argument. Madame Belle repeated her suggestion they tidy up and clear out. John Paul said he'd have a Mex shoeshine boy he knew wire Del Rio, asking them to reply in care of the cantina across from the ferry landing and thus leaving nothing for any smart-ass private investigators to trace back to them or the boarding-house.

Out in the hall, as they started for the stairs, Tom Corrigan stopped them, pointing down at the rug near the door to the now empty room as he snorted, "Aw, now ain't that precious!"

Madame Belle asked what he was talking about, or doing, as the man in white linen hunkered down to replace the match stem Longarm had wedged in the bottom hinge to show whether anyone had been in his room while he was out.

Repairing the damage, Corrigan rose back to his feet with a smile to say, "That boy's an old pro, no matter which side of the law he rides on. I sure hope he's really out on the Owlhoot Trail. For we might have use for a really experienced sinner."

"*Mais* what if we find out he is nobody important or, *sacre bleu*, an agent of the powers that be?"

Tom Corrigan was smiling, but he didn't sound too jovial as he told her, "In either case we'll have to do him in. If he's a damn bounty hunter he deserves to die. If he's just an innocent pilgrim running away to sea I've still got a bone to pick with him for sassing me. He called my hand downstairs, and nobody calls the hand of this child unless he's got at least a little blood on his own!"

Chapter 7

As they did at the bigger seaports of London, New York and of course New Orleans, seagoing vessels putting into the Tex-Mex port of Brownsville-Matamors sailed a good ways up a river estuary to tie up along a bewildersome tangle of docks, drydocks, and quays running along the river instead of jutting out into the same. A cobblestone *embarcadero* or waterfront service road ran betwixt the forest of ship masts and a jumble of cantinas, chander's shops, flophouses, warehouses and, of course, whorehouses catering to the seafaring trade.

Longarm had never made the mental adjustments required to pay for pussy and if he had, he was still feeling the effects of that steamboat ride aboard Miss Lava. So he almost strode on past the sultry young thing holding up a lamppost with the back seam of her flamenco outfit as she softly purred *"¿A dónde vas, El Brazo Largo?"*

Then he recalled how *Brazo Largo* translated to Long Arm and swung back to reply in his rusty Border Mex, "Never mind where I'm going and if you know what some of my friends call me, down Mexico way, you'll know how they'll feel about you telling anyone you ever saw me tonight?"

The whore looked hurt and pouted. "Must you insult me by warning me not to shit on my mother's grave, *El Brazo Largo*? What person party to *La Causa de Mejico Libre* would breathe a word about a friend of her people where the informers of *Los Rurales*, just across the river, might be listening? I only addressed you in the hope I could be of some small service to you. I am called *La Gitana*. I was told about you by a more important member of *La Causa* you may recall as *La Mariposa*."

Longarm smiled down at the one they called The Gypsy to allow he had fond memories indeed of her chum, Miss Butterfly. It was all right to call a *gal* a butterfly in Border Mex. It only meant a swishy queer if you said it to a guy.

He didn't ask how or where that rebel gal the gypsy gal cited might or might not be, that evening. You got along better with the dedicated Mex resistance movement when you didn't ask about anything you didn't just have to know about. Longarm didn't consider himself as much a part of *La Causa Mejico Libre* as Mexicans on both sides seemed to take him for. As a live-and-let-live American citizen, he had no vote in just who was running Mexico. But as a West-By-God-Virginia boy who'd grown up hating bullies and injustice, he'd somehow never had much luck in getting along with the riders for the current Mex dictatorship of El Presidente Porfirio Diaz. So heaps of Mex rebels, sharing the same views, tended to accept any *Yanqui loco* who'd wipe out a Mexican army column as one of their own. His modest protestations that he'd only done what he had to whilst riding for his *Tio* Sam south of the border had fallen on deaf ears.

So he knew he could trust *La Gitana* to keep word of his being in town to herself. Then he had a better notion and smiled thoughtfully down at the pretty little thing to

58

say there was something she might do for him.

La Gitana fluttered her lashes coyly and said, "Name it! Anything but up my *culo*! I do not really enjoy it there with any man and *La Mariposa* says you are hung like a *caballo!*"

Longarm sighed and said, "I wish gals wouldn't kiss and tell. That ain't what I want from you, Miss Gypsy. As you must have guessed, I'm down this way on business. Since you do business along this *embarcadero*, what have you heard about hiring paid assassins in these parts, lately?"

La Gitana shrugged and said, "Is easy to have someone killed, at any time, since that *chingado* General Diaz stole our *revolución* from our beloved Benito Juarez while the body was still warm. Desperate ones all along the border live from hand to mouth, ready to flee either way as your rangers and our *rurales* hunt them. For enough to get by another day, more than one of them would murder his own brother or sell his own mother's honor to a pig, if the pig had any money to offer."

Longarm said, "I'm not interested in your average border *buscadero*. They tell me there's a more professional . . . *agencia*, where you can apply to have someone killed in ways that can never be traced back to you. As I understand it, the assassin who does the deed never knows the name of the customer ordering the service. He or she pays some . . . I suppose you'd say *contratist*, who acts as a go-between. Have you heard of such services being available here in Brownsville?"

La Gitana shrugged and said, "You can find someone to perform any service on either side of the river, from *aborto* to *zalameria*. You may be looking for a woman of mystery called *La Dama Tigra*, who can tell fortunes and make some come true, *muy pronto*, for a few dollars more. That is all I know about her."

Longarm nodded thoughtfully as he mused, "That *would* be playing it close to the vest. Say you tell this fortune-telling Tiger Lady about a rich relation that's taking forever to pass on, a business rival or the one who stole your true love and she just *predicts* your worries may soon be over if you'd care to cross her palm with a little extra silver! One killer I seem to have traced back to this border town specialized in picking 'fair fights' he always seemed to win. I'm hoping they'll be in the market for similar skills, now that he's about to hang. So here's what I'd like you to do . . ."

La Gitana said she'd be proud to spread rumors along the *embarcadero* for a pal and so before he got back to the boardinghouse the news had proceeded him that the notorious Mormon Mike Mason, a participant in the recent Lincoln County War, out New Mexico way, had been spotted in Brownsville, wearing his six-gun and asking dumb questions about signing on most anything with sails as a green but willing deckhand.

Nobody at the boardinghouse had much to say to him when he got back just short of midnight. The only one he met was young Monique, who came to the front door when he found it locked for the night and twisted the bell knob. Monique told him she'd been starting to worry about him. The other boarders and Madame Belle had been upstairs a spell.

He told her he'd been talking to some pals he knew from other times and places, slipped her a dime for her trouble, and went on up to his hired room to inspect that match stem he'd wedged in the door hinge.

The match stem was in place, but not in the position he'd placed it in. Longarm smiled thinly as he unlocked the door, struck a light, and made sure they'd tidied up after going through his possibles. Then he shut the door behind him and, seeing there was enough light from outside to get by, shook out the match and undressed in the dark but not total darkness to get under just one sheet, bare-ass, since the gulf was too far downstream for the sea breezes to do that much good.

He had to toss the sheet aside and lie there wishing it was cooler as he tried to catch some shut-eye, knowing he'd never sleep worth mention once the Gulf Coast summer sun came up again. But despite his recent wanderings and all that exercise aboard that steamboat down from Laredo, he hadn't seen enough action to put a naturally active man in good shape to sleep that early on such a sweltersome night.

He was about to give up and get up when there came a flash of lightning through the jalousie slats, followed by a clap of thunder and the astounding splatters of a tropical downpour as it suddenly got ten or more degrees cooler inside.

"That's more like it," Longarm decided, plumping up his pillow and laying his head back down as he decided he was sort of tired after all. The streetlamp out front was blown out or drowned by the wind and rain off the gulf. So he lay there in total darkness punctuated by sudden glares of chalk-white electric light, way brighter than any of those new Edison bulbs they'd installed at the Cheyenne Social Club of late.

It was during an interval of total darkness, between thunderclaps, that he heard a gentle tapping at his door.

Knowing that whoever it was, it couldn't be a raven, Longarm rolled out of bed to draw his .44-40 from the holster hanging from a bedpost to pad over to the door on bare feet and murmur, "Who's there? I've been in bed and I ain't dressed for company."

A shemale whisper replied, "Let me in before somebody sees me out here in my nightgown, M'sieu. What may there be for either of us to see, unless you light the bedlamp, *hein*?"

So Longarm opened the door to her, murmuring, "I was sort of hoping you might care to join me, Miss Monique."

Then she was all over him and he had a time barring the door once more and hanging up his six-gun with her kneeling on the rug like so to fondle and kiss his suddenly inspired organ grinder.

Reaching down to lift her atop the bedstead with him, Longarm told her, "You have my undivided attention, girl. Let's not waste any of it anywhere but where I really want it!"

So she didn't argue as he rolled her on her back and lifted the hem of her silk nightgown out of the way as he forked a leg over to spread her thighs and then some.

There seemed to be more to young Monique than met the eye, he found, as he lowered himself aboard her exited flesh and guided the head of his questing shaft where they both seemed to want it to go. She thrust up to meet him as he entered her warm, wet innards. Then damned if she didn't bite down hard with her love muscles and sort of suck it up her as they kissed, French, with considerable experience, considering how young Monique looked, standing up with her duds on.

They soon had her nightgown all the way off and her big soft tits were another pleasant surprise. But he wasn't certain of his dawning suspicions until there came another lighting flash to reveal her wild-eyed face as she rolled her head back and forth in passion while she bumped and ground with her nails dug into his bare behind.

As they were plunged once more into cool damp darkness, Longarm almost asked Madame Belle Lasalle to what he owed such an honor. But it would have been

62

rude to tell a lady you were screwing that you'd thought you were screwing somebody else, and he was pretty certain of her reasons, albeit from the way she was panting in passion he suspected she had to be enjoying it almost as much as he was.

It didn't sound romantic, but as many a happily married couple could admit, if they ever admitted such private matters, experienced adults could enjoy coming with somebody they were sore at or, worse yet, just didn't care a fig about. Whores laughed at Johns who seemed to enjoy their favors, whilst Johns laughed at whores for giving them favors they couldn't ask from any woman who was likely to wind up kissing their grandchildren with those same lips.

Knowing it was a more serious game than casual slap-and-tickle betwixt two ships passing in the night, Longarm put his back and all he could keep hard into the older woman who was out to gain his confidence.

He knew how sincerely she was really grinding back when she moaned aloud, "Oh, don't stop, Mormon Mike! For, *mon Dieu* I am about to fly over *la lune* once more!"

He pounded harder, as most men would have, until he, at any rate, had sincerely shot his wad inside her. Then, as they lay cuddled atop the rumpled bedding with the rain lashing the jalousies to cool them down, Longarm asked in a hesitant voice why she'd called him Mormon Mike. He said, "I'm just a plain old Mike, from out New Mexico way. I don't know nothing about them Latterday Saints around the Great Salt Lake."

She soothed, "If you say so, *mon cher*. Let us rest a bit and perhaps we can manage another *zigzig* before I must creep back to my own room. It would never do for my servants to learn I have no character. You must consider me a dirty old woman, too, *hein*?"

He said, "Aw, you ain't that old, Miss Belle, and I

reckon I've just been as dirty as anybody around here."

She sighed and said, "I know I should behave myself. *Mais* I am not yet old enough to have no feelings and my married life was so unjust. Could we share a cigarette as we talk, *mon cher?* I have a packet of Turkish tobacco Fatimas somewhere on the floor, now, thanks to your most passionate approach!"

She was really good at what she was up to. But Longarm had questioned suspects in his own time. So he casually replied, "I don't smoke. You go ahead if you want to. I don't mind others smoking. I just never picked up the habit, for some reason. How come you said your married life was unjust? Did your man beat you, fool around, or fail to satisfy you?"

She sighed and said, "We had perhaps twenty good years, in bed and out. He liked my cooking as well. Then he came down with a species of cancer and for a long, distressing time he could neither enjoy my . . . cooking or . . . *merde alors*, why am I telling all this to anyone else? One has to be there, nursing a dying man day after endless day, before one can even guess at the mixed emotions one feels. *Eh bien*, at last he died, leaving me this property, at least."

It would have been dumb to ask if she'd had her fortune told by any Tiger Ladies whilst she waited for a slowly dying man to go on and get it over with. He'd heard that part of the story before. Albeit there was no just cause to suspect any of the other kith and kin stuck in such a situation of having taken steps to speed the process.

She decided she'd rather puff on him than a Turkish cigarette and so they wound up too busy to talk much more before she allowed she had to get back to her own room and slipped out of his. With him only hoping he'd satisfied her in more ways than one.

He had. Madame Belle didn't go back to her own room. She joined Tom Corrigan in his room, saying as she stripped, "If he's not a Mormon his acting skills are *tres formidable*. He naturally denied it when I tried to get him to admit he was really Mormon Mike. *Mais* he insisted on calling Mormons Latterday Saints, as Mormons, themselves, prefer to be described. Need I say how anxious he was to smoke with me during a little pillow talk?"

The burly older man on the bedcovers, not wearing his Panama suit or anything else, patted the mattress beside him to say, "Come and set by my side ere you leave me and I'll let you smoke all you want with me, afterwards."

Madame Belle Lasalle giggled girlishly for a woman her age. Few men felt too sure of their own virility to be jealous and it made her feel deliciously dirty to get in bed with one man with the seed of another still warm and wet inside her.

But it was not to be, for the moment. For there came some urgent rapping on Corrigan's door and the big Irishman trimmed the bedlamp to rise in the dark and open up for Juan Pablo Jones.

The Tex-Mex joined them in the dark to pant, "I have just come from that cantina near the Western Union. The sheriff's department of Val Verde County just wired an answer to the message we sent upstream as the mysterious Mike Carpenter and, *caramba*, you'll never in this world guess what they just told us about that *estafador malo*!"

Chapter 8

As Longarm had bet when he'd planted the seeds of Mormon Mike Mason, the wire they'd sent to the late Eagle Emerson of Del Rio had confused the shit out of everyone there. So Juan Pablo Jones told his own side down in Brownsville, "The sheriff wired back. Demanding to know what Mike Carpenter had ever worked for that Emerson outfit whilst they were still in business, according to old Eagle Emerson's widow."

Tom Corrigan frowned in the dark as the wind and rain came down outside and thoughtfully asked, "Do either of you recall the dates on those reward posters our mysterious Mike has in his own room down the hall?"

Madame Belle volunteered, "There was no dateline. They simply asked for information leading to the capture of Mormon Mike Mason, wanted for questioning about gunplay from Utah Territory to Val Verde County, Texas."

Juan Pablo Jones said, "According to the sheriff of the same, old Eagle Emerson was shot dead in his office just a few weeks ago by some person or persons unknown."

Corrigan decided, "It fits. Mormon Mike didn't want

to be questioned and helped himself to some reward poster on his way out!"

That was only partly true. Longarm had recalled the recent unsolved killing of an old pal of Marshal Vail's who'd gone into business for himself up Del Rio way. But, as he'd bet his own hide, truth and fiction fit together tight enough to satisfy a border tough so confident of his own superiority that he invited Juan Pablo to join him and the Madame for a three-in-the-tub celebration.

So even if her eyes were hard as ever, Madame Belle's soft olive features were glowing some as she presided at the head of her breakfast table off the central hall the next morning. Longarm saw there were six other boarders in addition to the blustering Corrigan and Juan Pablo Jones, who for some reason couldn't seem to meet his eye that morning. There was no way to tell, even if he asked, whether any of her other boarders were in on anything with her. Five of them were men of indeterminate age and occupation. The other gal at the table had her mousy hair pinned up, wore a summer frock of raw silk the color of a new throw-rope and seemed to have nothing to say. After that she was built mighty fine, if you liked 'em on the slim side. Longarm felt a tad annoyed with himself as he caught himself undressing both her and Madame Belle with his eyes, idly wondering what it would be like to alternate in 'em, dog style. That was the trouble with cutting down on tobacco and strong drink at the same time. It left a man nothing to yearn for but wild, wild women.

Nobody said anything dirty, or sneaky, at the table. Once they'd finished the French toast and gumbo rice with red peppers and black beans Longarm excused himself before coffee was served and went out on the veranda, dying for a smoke as well, as he tested the morning air and decided they were in for another clam-bake.

Tom Corrigan came out to join him, wearing a fresh shirt under that same rumpled linen and smoking a fucking Havana Claro, or a fair immitation of the same.

Longarm had been along the Gulf of Mexico in high summer before. So he remained on his feet to catch such stray air currents as might come his way and avoid sitting in his own sweat. Corrigan leaned over the veranda rail to say, "Just been reading me some interesting telegraph wires. Pal of ours wired he'll be headed down this way, now that things have cooled down some. They call him Bunny Weed on account of his hare lip. Weed's just his family name, or so he says. I hope he knows what he's doing. We're pretty sure he was recently face-to-face with that famous lawman, Longarm."

Longarm shrugged and easily answered, "Ain't no skin off my ass." And this was the simple truth, once you saw through the clumsy trickery. Longarm had known from the beginning that the description he'd made up for Mormon Mike Mason fit the way he was usually described, truthfully, in those infernal newspaper stories about a man just trying to do his job. So if he hadn't been dead-certain Bunny Weed and his smaller sidekick were both dead and burnt beyond recognition he might have worried more about an owlhoot rider who knew the real Longarm on sight showing up to expose him.

Since Bunny Weed wasn't about to, Longarm aka Mike Carpenter said, "It's sure fixing to heat up and that infernal Spanish Dancer ain't due for the near future. I was asking around the docks last night."

Corrigan blew expensive cigar smoke at him thoughtfully as he asked, "Is that where you were so late? You never said which side you were on out Lincoln County way, Mike."

Longarm replied, "I understand they got these Hindu coolies over to British India. They call 'em pluck-a-wall-eyes on account they set outback plucking on a long cord to move a ceiling fan back and forth for the English folk inside. I doubt you'd ever get a Mex or free person of color to do that, here in Texas. Mebbe someday they'll invent some way to cool things off with steam power."

Corrigan insisted, "I asked you whether you'd fought for the Murphy-Dolan faction or Tunstall and McSween. I've a friendly reason for asking, Mike."

Longarm decided, "That newfangled electric power would be cooler. It seems to me that when you can send messages for miles or light up your nights with electricity there ought to be some way to cool things down with the same. I don't see how Queen Victoria means to hold on to India if the white folk yonder cool themselves in hot weather with Hindu sweat. All the tidewater planters of Old Dixie asked of their help was some honest sweat as they sat in the shade and look how that turned out!"

Corrigan cursed him for a stubborn fool and said, "I'm trying to help you, Mike. To start with you don't want to call yourself Mike Carpenter anymore. The sheriff of Val Verde County has been asking about for a Mike Carpenter here in Brownsville. I know why you're on the run from Del Rio and I know how come you're so anxious to hop a sailing ship clean out of these United States. If I was you, I'd pick another first name as well and take up smoking, whether I inhaled or not!"

"I don't know what you're talking about," Longarm lied, adding, "I ain't done nothing to nobody up to Val Verde County, so why would any sheriff from there be after me?" And this, when you studied on it, cost his conscience nothing.

Corrigan said, "Yes, you do. And time's running out on you. We know you don't have enough money to book passage aboard a coastal steamer and have enough left to start all over, once you get where you ain't wanted. We know you're sure to be caught if you stay here in Brownsville running down your bankroll day by day. Were you paid a regular salary or were you working at piecework rates out New Mexico way?"

Longarm said, "I disremember. What does it matter whether I rode for either side in the sweet long-ago? All the major players are dead or run off. Tunstall, Brewer and McSween on the one side were shot dead. Sheriff Brady, Deputy Hindmen on the other side were shot, old Major Murphy died natural and Jim Dolan ain't been seen in recent memory."

"What about Billy the Kid?" asked Corrigan.

Longarm shrugged and said, "We were talking about major players. Dick Brewer commanded the Tunstall-McSween riders, 'til he was killed by Buckshot Roberts and vice versa. The Kid suffers from an easy-to-remember nickname. They say he's washing dishes down around Lordsburg these days. I wouldn't know. Why should I?"

The older man in white linen chuckled and said, "I'd have expected you to pick the winning side. But listen tight and quit playing cute with a pal who's only trying to help you. The sheriff of Val Verde County is asking around about Mike Carpenter. The talk along the waterfront is that Mormon Mike Mason is in town. How long can you hope to play a lone hand with a shrinking bankroll and nowhere to run?"

Longarm shrugged and said, "There's always somewheres to run. How come you want to be such a pal of mine, Tom?"

Corrigan said, "We may have more in common than you think. To begin with I used to have this other pal who was good at picking gunfights, and winning. He's been picked up by the law. He'll likely hang. So we need someone like him in our . . . organization. The two of you look nothing alike and poor old Solitaire was a lot more polite to me. But, as I understand it, the notorious Mormon Mike was rumored to pick lots of gunfights out New Mexico way and was wanted for questioning about some more recent ones in West Texas."

Longarm truthfully replied, "Nobody can prove I rode for either side in the Lincoln County War and I ain't wanted in Texas for nothing!"

Corrigan soothed, "Have it your way. Eagle Emerson only wanted to ask you about some gunplay up to Val Verde County when you, or somebody, blew his candle out. Let's not argue about ancient history. How would you like to make a fast five hundred dollars?"

"Who do I have to kill?" asked Longarm, in jest.

Corrigan's voice was dead serious as he replied, "A rich ranchero down Matamoros way. It's no concern of yours why someone else wants him dead. Doing him in ought to be right up your alley. He's one of them hoity-toity *hidalgos con sangre azul* with a coat of arms and silver braid all over his big sombrero. He struts around wearing a brace of ivory-handled Colt Presentation .45s and he's slapped leather on more than one lesser light who intimated that his shit might stink. Picking a fair fight with such a total asshole shouldn't be tough, for a man with a mouth like yours. How do you like it so far?"

Longarm stared up at the unfortunately clear sky to mutter, "We sure are going to sweat some, today. How do you propose a gringo might gun a big shot Mexican on his side of the border and get back on this side alive?"

"Matamoros law's been fixed, cheap. They don't like the strutting bastard, either. *Los Rurales*, patrolling betwixt towns as they do, don't have to know about the . . . fair fight before they read about it in the morning papers.

71

By that time you'll have caught the ferry back across the Rio Grande, or the Rio Bravo as they'll have the signs lettered on the south bank.

Longarm said, "I know the Mexicans call it the Rio Bravo. I'm more worried about getting back across a rose by any name. It sounds like a sucker's play, to me. How do I know I'll be paid, even if I make it back in one piece?"

Corrigan said, "You get half on agreeing to the contract. You get another two-fifty when you're back alive and well on this side of the river, with him stone dead on the other. I know what you're worried about, Mormon Mike. You're afraid we might be trying to get that Mex done in at bargain rates. You're wondering if we don't mean to send you after him with a down payment, let you finish him off for . . . our clients, and abandon you to the wolves."

"The thought had occurred to me," said Longarm, dryly.

Corrigan sighed and said, "It's such suspicions that make good help so hard to find in our line of work. Wouldn't it be dumb for anyone to go to all the trouble of scouting up and recruiting a real pro?"

"It happens," Longarm grumbled, adding, "I ain't saying I know any of this from personal experience but the fact remains that after promising hope-to-die-with-sugar-on-it to Dick Brewer's so called Regulators, Uncle John Chisum never paid them shit for gunning Sheriff Brady and they were on their own, once the new governor stepped in to calm things down with federal troops. Few of the gun waddies who'd risked their asses for the Murphy-Dolan faction ever got more than a pat on the same, either!"

"That so-called war was a business dispute amongst amateurs," the self-confessed professional insisted.

The trouble was, as Longarm saw things, that he'd never prove a thing in court unless he went along with the murder of some Mexican he'd never be able to name unless he agreed to the crime!

So he agreed to the crime, as a real gun-for-hire would have, knowing he could always back out at the very last minute, providing that snotty Mex blue-blood let him.

Running that notion around the track some more, Longarm asked who they wanted him to pick a fight with, where they wanted him to pick the fight and, more importantly, when he'd get to see some money.

Corrigan said, "Later. This has just been an opening move, to find out whether you might want in or out. I have to go over the fine print of the contract with . . . somebody I work for. I'm just a dealer. I don't run the casino, see?"

Longarm was commencing to. The mastermind or -minds behind this murdersome operation was hiding inside layers of onion skin whilst they, in turn, would be nigh impossible to convict of doodly toad squat. For how was an arresting officer to sell a judge and jury on "Nobody told me who I was working for or the name of any clients who wanted me to pick a fight with some bird" when the defense was sure to ask if you'd ever been given direct orders to kill anybody for any particular reason.

Tom Corrigan was saying, "You're so right about how hot it's got out here already. Why don't you scout up some shade whilst I confirm the deal with . . . somebody? We can talk about it some more at noon, when Madame Belle serves up our dinners."

Longarm didn't argue. The older man in white linen went back inside to confer with Madame Belle if she was the Tiger Lady, or with somebody else if she wasn't.

Longarm stood there alone for another minute or so.

Then he went down the veranda steps to stroll over to the waterfront in search of something time-killing. Time took a heap of killing on a Gulf Coast morn when you weren't allowed to smoke or drink and it was too blamed hot to consider coming.

He spied a newsstand by the ferry landing and ambled over to see if they had any magazines he might want to read.

They didn't. He'd read most of the issues on sale and felt no call to read fashion magazines and such he'd already passed on.

Then he noticed their rack of out-of-town newspapers and a headline off the *Del Rio Democrat* caught his eye—a lot.

He dropped the two cents in the newsdealer's tray and hauled the upstream edition out to unfold it all the way and make certain. Then he cussed so hard the old newsdealer shot him a funny look.

They'd arrested the killer of Edgar (Eagle) Emerson the private dick, according to the *Del Rio Democrat*. Old Eagle hadn't been shot at his desk by any out-of-town desperado. The killer, according to the sheriff who'd just arrested him at home, had been a local dentist who's wife had hired Emerson to get the goods on him and his receptionist-nurse. He'd been caught, of course, when he tried to break things off with his other woman and she'd naturally turned him in with an unsigned poison pen letter. So they had her in jail as well, and the two former lovers were accusing one another of everything but decency.

Longarm folded the paper with the fussy care of a man who wasn't certain what he meant to do with it, muttering, "Jesus H. Christ. What do we do now?"

Chapter 9

Longarm made sure he got back to the boardinghouse well before dinnertime and sat on the veranda steps with the folded newspaper beside his denim-clad rump. He was glad he was wearing no more than jeans and an open hickory shirt as he took off his Stetson, wiped the leather band with his kerchief, and sat it on its telescope top to air beside the paper.

He was dying for a smoke, but Mormon Mike didn't smoke and he'd been trying to cut down in any case. So he promised himself a box of Havana Perfectos as soon as this was over.

Longarm had long since noticed that our less grown-up parts resented being told they couldn't have something that they hungered for whatever it was you wouldn't give 'em. Longarm just hated that prissy three-piece suit they'd made him buy when President Hayes took over with his prissy desk code for federal employees. Yet Longarm knew that if they told him he'd never in his life get to wear a suit and tie again, he'd miss that itchy tobacco tweed like fire. So he told himself he'd spring for a whole private can of Arbuckle brand ready-ground coffee to go with those fine cigars and tried to hunger for other pleasures instead.

That got easier when his mousy fellow boarder with the trim figure came up the walk, looking sort of wilted as she fanned her hatless head with her own straw boater. But she smelled more of lavender water than sweat as she paused long enough to remark on how hot it was and ask him if they were fixing to have more of that icky Cajun grub for dinner.

Longarm rose, having been raised by poor but proper parents, to say, "I suspect *Creole* is the term you have in mind, Miss . . . ?"

"Oakhurst. Velma Oakhurst," she replied.

So he said, "I'd be Mike Carpenter, then. I'm sure Miss Belle and her help describe themselves as *Creole*— French-speaking folk born in the West Indies or around the Gulf of Mexico. Cajuns are another bunch entire, deported from French Arcadia, up Nova Scotia way, after one of them French and Indian wars and resettled around the mouths of the Mississippi. I found this out when I was working a . . . just visiting New Orlean a spell back. Folk in them parts can get mighty sniffy when outsiders fail to note distinctions. Albeit, to tell the truth, Creoles and Cajuns don't seem all that different to me."

"What's that slimey stuff they cook with?" she sighed.

He said, "Gumbo, ma'am. From the green pods of this African flower called okra. I'll allow it takes some getting used to. But if you just remember it's sort of thick sap from a plant instead of slime from a critter it's easier to ignore it. How do you like Tex-Mex, or Chinese?"

She said, "I grew up in Penn State. I could dine forever on Madame Belle's gumbo before I'd care for all that red pepper and odd smells. I've never had any Chinese food. I've heard some of it's sort of tasty."

Longarm nodded and said, "It can be, if you know

what to order. As in all cooking, some Chinese dishes taste better than others. I ain't sure I'll be here at suppertime. I may have to go across the river for a spell. But if I'm still here, or when I get back, how would you like to try some Pork Lo Mein with me at this Chinese place I noticed down the *embarcadero* a ways, after dark, when it don't hurt so much to set still at a table?"

She fluttered her lashes, started to say no, then allowed she'd need time to study on it. It turned out she worked at a bookstore not too far off and, meanwhile, meant to take a cool bath and change her duds before dinner. So she went inside and Longarm sat back down, glad to have something other than black coffee and a smoke to crave.

He suspected part of the craving folk felt for members of the other sex was inspired by the challenge. You could eat too much, drink too much or smoke yourself sick without having to talk anyone else into a thing, as long as you could pay a nominal sum to overindulge. But he'd read about this South Pacific island where everyone ran about naked as jays and screwed each other freely, with no rules at all about such matters. So naturally they had all sorts of dos and don'ts, they called them taboos, about what you could eat, who you could eat, and who you could eat most anything or anybody with. So those poor South Sea folk went about all day and night thinking about food instead of the bare tits and asses all around.

But thinking about the tits and trim ass hidden under Velma's damp summerweight silk served to take his mind off warm sticky gumbo with no coffee to wash it on down. So what the hell.

Tom Corrigan was wearing the same rumpled white linen as he came home for dinner, or mayhaps on other business. Longarm felt no call to rise for him. Corrigan sat down beside him on the steps, gasping, "Lord have mercy, ain't this cold spell something? I just heard something you might find interesting, or distressing. Word's gotten around about Mormon Mike being in town. I just now heard one of the whores at Madame Rosie's parlor house claims to know the famous gunslick personal, in the biblical sense. If I was a gunslick on the dodge I'd steer clear of parlor houses. First place the law looks when they hear a want might be about."

Longarm handed the older man the out-of-town paper, trying to sound triumphant as he chortled, "A lot you know. Read this here *Del Rio Democrat* before you go accusing me of gunning anyone in Val Verde County."

As Corrigan spread the paper to scan the front page, Longarm added, "I don't hang about whorehouses, neither. I'm too pretty. Whores are always bragging they've serviced Frank and Jesse, too. Ain't sure I know any whores here in Brownsville."

Corrigan read on to the end of the article before he nodded to himself and said to Longarm, "The gal at Madame Rosie's says she came down the river with you, screwing all the way. Claims she screwed you earlier, further west, when you took her away from Billy the Kid."

Longarm snorted incredulously and said, truthfully, "She made that part up from whole cloth. She was no more than an old pal I knew from this border town up the river and I was afraid she'd kiss and tell when we met up aboard that steamboat. But you know how it is when a traveling man has time and space to kill and hasn't had any lately."

Corrigan set the paper aside to say, "So she knows you from up Del Rio way and our Lord and the sheriff of Val Verde County sure has been smiling on you, Mike. It seems you're fixing to get away with Murder Most Foul by shithouse luck!"

"Says in the paper they've arrested somebody else for

gunning old Eagle Emerson up yonder," Longarm insisted, paying out some more rope for Corrigan's self-assurance to hang itself with.

The man in white linen snorted, "Well, sure, they had to arrest *somebody* and there must not have been any strange tramps in their drunk tank. That poor dentist was turned in by a woman scorned. You don't have to swat a fly to be accused of murder, rape and sodomy by a gal you've deserted in favor of your wife. Since they've traced her poison pen letter back to her, she's more likely to go to jail than him, if he has a lawyer worth shit. Ain't a shred of evidence saying Eagle Emerson couldn't have been gunned in his office, private, by others he'd been investigating, such as a certain gun-for-hire I just now found a job for."

Longarm stared out into the dusty, sunbaked distance as he quietly replied, "Not for free. When do I see the front money and where do I pick up the final payment?"

Corrigan said, "Matamoros. Before and after. No money changes hands and nothing gets done on this side of the border, under Texas jurisdiction."

He pulled out a folded sheet of foolscap and passed it to Longarm as he added, "There's just no saying who typed up these instructions if you're picked up or try to double-cross us. All I know, your honor, is that somebody handed me this paper and asked me to pass it on to another boarder I knew to howdy. I never read it."

Longarm opened the sheet, scanned the few sentences, and replied, "Says I'm to go to this *Cantina del Camino Real* near the ferry landing on the far side, order me some *tonica*, and say nothing when somebody hands me an envelope."

"Does it now?" asked Tom Corrigan innocently.

Longarm nodded and said, "That's all they wrote. Pretty slick. An envelope from someone I can't identify on this side of the border, holds the front money and further instruction on the Mex side. What if I'm picked up by *Los Rurales* before I can get rid of the evidence?"

Corrigan replied in a mocking falsetto, "*Por favor me Magistrado*, I had no idea what might be in the sealed envelope I was asked to give to that gringo and I am only twelve years old."

Longarm didn't feel half as casual as he tried to sound, asking when they wanted him to head for the ferry landing.

The older man said, "Evening rush, with greasers working on this side headed home for supper might be best. You'd be just another face in the crowd, getting off the ferry south of the border. You'll want to drift into that cantina in the tricky light around sundown and order that unusual drink for a gringo standing at the end of the bar closer to the front door. When this street kid slips in with an offer to shine your boots, don't refuse him. That's all I have to say about the matter. I have no idea why they wanted my fellow boarder to act so strange, your honor."

Longarm handed the typed instructions back, saying, "You might feel even safer once you've burnt this. I can remember the time and place to have my boots shined well enough."

Corrigan allowed it was a pleasure to work with professionals and got up to go inside. Longarm sat out front as others came home for dinner, without a one of them allowing he was enjoying the weather. Then one of the maids sounded her three-toned chimes and he had to go on inside for what turned out to be a right sensible noon meal of cold cuts and what Madame Belle described as "fromage." It looked and tasted like plain old rat-trap cheese to Longarm.

Nobody had much to say as they et and ran, the dining

room being a whole lot hotter than their uncooked meal with iced coffee.

Passing on the coffee had hurt like blazes. Longarm could smell the French chickory in the tinkling glasses, but he hadn't had any coffee of any description since before he'd turned into Mormon Mike and he was wondering if that was why he had a mild headache.

He didn't need a bout of coffee nerves. He had enough to feel nervous about. The instructions to order plain tonic water might mean they'd accepted him as the imaginary Mormon Mike. If they had not, they'd have him south of the border when they made their move. If they were on to who he might really be, they'd know there was a Mexican bounty posted in *El Brazo Largo*, a pain-in-the-ass gringo *El Presidente* had a bone to pick with.

The mousy-haired and nicely built Velma Oakhurst caught up with him on the veranda, to say, "I have to get back to my bookshop, now. But I've been thinking about that Chinese restaurant you mentioned. I don't see how any dining room could be stuffier than the one inside. So let me think about it some more and we'll see, when I get off this evening."

Longarm ruefully told her he'd be out of town on business of his own by that time. Then, to recover any ground he'd just lost, he told her he'd walk her to her bookstore and mayhaps find something to read for later.

She dimpled up at them that they were in business to sell books and never asked him about his own business. So that was another point in her favor as he idly wondered whether she had mouse-colored hair all over.

It was too early, and too hot, to ask. As he walked her around the first corner they came to, inland to a more fashionable avenue lined with shops catering to ladies who'd never go near the *embarcadero* without a male escort of some size, he idly asked Velma how come the

81

place she worked didn't follow the local Tex-Mex cus-toms of *la siesta*, seeing it got just as hot and slow for everyone in those parts betwixt noon and say three or four when the sun got to casting shadows some more.

She said the place she worked was run by a Boston chain and didn't seem to know much about *la siesta*. She held it was a lazy Mex notion that wasted the better part of the day.

As they strolled along in the muggy heat, Longarm explained, "Them sultry hours betwxit high noon and shade along one side of every street hardly qualify as the better parts of any day, Miss Velma. As you may have noticed, Tex-Mex enterprises don't lose as many business hours as you might expect by following hot weather rules. They make up for *la siesta* when it's too hot to do business by staying open past midnight, when it's cooler, and all their competition from up north has been shut down for hours. I know that I, for one, would rather get a haircut or try on new boots after dark in this neck of the woods."

"Or take a lady off for a Chinese supper in the cool of evening?" she softly inquired.

They were fixing to have a full moon that evening, too, cuss Corrigan for a spoilsport.

But he hadn't been sent all this way in high summer to admire moonlight on the Rio Grande with well-built mousy-haired gals.

So when they got to her shop to find its door locked with a sign behind the glass telling everyone they were closed for lunch and meant to be back by one P.M. she told him as she unlocked it how she ran the place alone. So as she hung her boater out of the way and got things in order by the cash till Longarm perused her stacks to pick out three non-fiction tomes he'd read about in the book reviews of the *Denver Post*. As he took them to the

82

counter to pay for them the mousy-haired Velma marveled, "Good heavens, *Geology, Recently Found Cliff Dwellings* and a *Migratory Birds West of the Mississippi*? You are a heavy reader, Mister Carpenter!"

He shrugged and said, "I can't say I understand all the words, but I never got to finish school and reading books like these helps me go to sleep."

She sighed and said, "I know what you mean. I prefer romantic novels for reading in bed, but for some reason, they just as often keep me awake, or worse yet, inspire disturbing dreams."

As she placed his purchases in a paper bag for him he didn't ask her what sort of dreams a body might have after reading a romantic novel alone in bed. He knew. That was why he prefered non-fiction for his lonesome reading, late at night in a strange town.

Chapter 10

The awesome heat was broken by an awful thunderstorm that afternoon. The only time the weather was really pleasant on the Gulf Coast was the day after a hurricane. But it was too early in the summer to hope for a hurricane.

Crossing on the ferry in his shirtsleeves just the same, Longarm figured he'd blended in enough as two Mex gals standing near him in the bows went on about *chingago gringo* bosses who expected sensible servants to *work* during *la siesta*. He'd spied few other Anglo faces in the tricky light aboard the evening ferry. Nobody on the far shore gave a shit as the crowd steamed off. The Mexican dictatorship taxed anything of value going *out* of the country. They were pleased as punch to have *Yanqui* dollars coming *in*.

The cobbles were still wet in low spots as Longarm made his way to the nearby *Cantina del Camino Real*. So his well broken-in army boots were a tad soggy for shining as he bellied up to the bar inside and, ignoring the looks he seemed to be catching, ordered the sort of *tonica* it was all right for a Latter Day Saint to drink.

He paid but didn't drink the tall glass of fizz-water the barmaid slid across the fake mahogany to him. He didn't see any shoeshine boys but, as he wearily awaited, a nineteen- or-twenty-year-old bravo in split bell-bottom fancy pants, a big straw sombrero and a Starr .38 worn low and sidedraw peeled off from the cheering section along the back wall to sidle up to Longarm with an oily smile, marveling, *"Ay, que muchacho,* does your mother know you are out, drinking *tonica* without some *cerveza* for to wash it down? Maybe I will buy you some, if you do not have the *dinero* for to drink like an hombre, eh?"

Longarm quietly suggested, *"Vete. Si me haces una de tus pendejas, te voy a romper la cabeza chingada."*

The cantina tough blinked, blanched, and managed to call out in his thick accent, "Hey, it speaks Spanish! Most rudely, too! I offer for to drink with it and it threatens for to break my fucking head!"

The barmaid urgently hissed, "We have to talk, Ernesto. Move down this way with me while I have a word with you. I promise you will thank me, later."

So they moved down the bar to whisper about him as Longarm got back to worrying about more important matters. He didn't have enough on any of them to make one arrest. Billy Vail hadn't sent him down that way to get his fool self arrested for murder. So how was he supposed to get out of killing some fool Mex without failing this obvious test? He knew he could simply walk away from the case, leaving that Solitaire Stryker's mission to Denver way in the middle of the air. Longarm was pretty certain, now, this bunch he'd just been scouting the edges of had ordered Stryker up yonder to kill somebody important. Since nobody important had been killed before Stryker had been recognized and turned in, Longarm was forced to weigh the advantages and disadvantages of swapping a dead Mex for one saved fellow citizen.

He knew he couldn't do it. Once a lawman got to bending the law that much he wasn't a lawman anymore. He was just another bad man with a badge.

Longarm knew there were all too many of the same in his line of work. Some held you fought fire with fire and Mister Charlie Dickins hadn't been the first and wouldn't be the last to decribe the law as assinine. A heap of laws were uninforcible and as many more were just plain silly. But whilst Longarm was inclined to bend some laws and pay no mind to chickenshit, he knew a lawman who'd kill a man to catch folk who killed others would not only make him as bad as they were but justify their logic. Nobody killed anybody for no reason. So there was no way to claim his reason would be any better than their own. He had to figure something out, sudden as hell. For in the front door came a dirty-faced barefoot boy with a shoeshine box in one hand and a fat hemp paper envelope in the other.

The kid didn't look at Longarm. He didn't look at the soda water on the bar. He looked at the barmaid and she looked at Longarm. The kid came over and handed him the envelope. Longarm asked how much he wanted to shine his boots. The kid told him to shove his boots up his ass and lit out faster than he'd entered.

Longarm put the envelope inside his shirt, unopened, and headed out the same door. He'd only gone a few yards along the lamplit walk in the gathering dusk before that *buscadero* in the big hat and Starr .38 caught up with him and shyly said, "*Un momento, por favor.* I wish it known I meant no disrespect to *El Señor* . . . or his friends."

It was important to know who they were talking about. If that Mex barmaid had him down as a hired gun, that was one thing. If she had him down as a lawman with pals in Mex rebel circles that was another. It worked both ways, with the odds in favor of her being in on something with Corrigan and that Tiger Lady, if there was anything to the sreet talk about a mysterious fortune-teller. He was pretty certain that barmaid had fingered him for that messenger boy with the shoeshine kit. But she could have been wondering what *El Brazo Largo* was going to do or say next.

He asked the young jasper who'd followed him outside, "How are you called? I'll pass on your respects to those friends of mine you meant no disrespect to."

The cantina tough quickly replied he didn't want his fortune told and crawfished away in the tricky light.

Longarm circled until he was sure nobody was tailing him. Then he sat at a blue wooden table under the awning of a sidewalk *café* and ordered *und merienda* to give himself an excuse to sit under their awning lanterns undisturbed for the moment.

As he nibbled his ration of light snacks he opened the thick tan envelope and put the U.S. Treasury silver certificates away without counting his advance payment. The terse typewritten instructions that went with the money told him a certain Don Hernan Vasquez Padilla was expected to ride in from his *hacienda* down the *Camino Real* to pay a call on his mistress, at a town house he kept her in for his convenience. Both addresses were given. The not-too-detailed instructions told Longarm the rich rancher and his play-pretty would be attending the wedding reception of a bullfighter old Vasquez owned a share in. It hardly needed to add that such occasions tended to get noisy and wild once the drinking of toasts and the dancing of flamencos got under way. Don Hernan was said to have a quick temper and a possessive attitude toward his mistress, his wife, his serving *chicas* and most any woman under his *proteccion*. He'd already killed more than one unfortunate for expressing no more than admiration for a gal he considered his own. He'd shot a *federale* officer for complimenting him on his taste in play-pretties. You got to carry on like that in Mexico under *El Presidente*, if you were rich enough and had your *peones* voting the right way.

There was one last address. When he touched the list to the candle flame on his table as he polished off a *tapa menudillo*, his waiter came over to ask how come.

Longarm explained he was burning a note he never wanted a certain husband to read. The waiter chuckled fondly and said he wished he was still young and foolish.

There seemed no way to work it there in town. That Tiger Lady and her pals would likely have someone watching the town house of that mistress and the hired hall where they'd be holding the big fandango. It was up for grabs whether the Don's wife, an admirer of the same, or the mistress, or mayhaps a bullfighter who wanted to own all of his fool self had paid to have the arrogant cuss killed. Longarm knew they had paid well over a thousand if he was to get five hundred. So somebody was anxious as all get-out to see the last of Don Hernan Vasquez Padilla.

Longarm had been in Matamoros before. So he knew where to go to hire a pinto barb, an exposed-tree dally-roping saddle and a bridle with a Spanish bit lest anyone else in these parts argue with him.

Then he rode out to the south along *El Camino Real*, as the royal post road of Spanish times had been described and never renamed after the Revolution of '21. There was an outside chance he could get his assigned target to listen to reason, provided he could talk to him in private before he rode in to get liquored up and proddy.

A still-sober Don Hernan might well see the advantages of hiding out a spell, where no paid assassins could get at him, until they could find out who'd paid said assassins off to get him.

Longarm knew that meant he was going to have to show his cards face-up to a rider for the current dictatorship, who sounded like a pain in the ass on his *own*!

But, in his day, Longarm had managed to make deals with Comanche, Apache and worse—even *Federales* and *Rurales*. Provided they were halfway sane, even dedicated bastards could be counted on to see when a deal was in their own best interests and he doubted Don Hernan was anxious to be murdered on orders of some secret enemy.

It took a spell to ride shed of Matamoros and the moon he'd had other plans for smiled brightly down on the coastal plains as he rode at a lope, anxious to head Don Hernan off before he could show himself alive and well in town.

Folk who knew Mexico from postcards and the printed covers of sheet music about *La Paloma* and such tended to picture all of it the way only its northern high country looked. There was plenty of cactus over on the west coast, true enough, but left to its drothers the eastern lowland of Mexico would have gone to ever-more lush jungle as you worked your way south, with the stretch betwixt, say, Matamoros and Vera Cruz as lushly forested as Florida. But as in the case of Old Spain, itself, the way Spanish-speaking folk raised and grazed livestock made for wide-open spaces supporting considerable herds of mostly black Nubian goats and originally North African longhorn cows the Moors had introduced to the plains of Spain. So the moonlit range to either side was mostly *llano* as they said in place of the French word, prairie, and looked much the same as the high plains up Colorado way, save for being carpet grass, centipede grass, Bermuda grass and such, with the scattered dark clumps of trees live-oak instead of box elder, chokecherry, cottonwood and such.

Nobody overtook him, riding faster than most on a cooler but hardly brisk summer evening. He avoided others riding into town by reining off the road and either ducking into some tree-shade or, caught in the open, trotting his livery pony at right angles to the highway as if on his way to somewheres else in the night.

He was only challenged once, and he'd ridden well off the road in the direction of a distant point of light by the time someone behind called out in Spanish, "Hey, *caballero,* we see you out there in the moonlight! Who are you and where do you think you are going at this hour, eh?"

Longarm didn't answer. He knew his accent would be remembered and had he wanted anyone to remember passing an Anglo on his way to *El Rancho Vasquez* he'd have never bothered to avoid them.

As he just kept going, neither heeling his mount faster nor reining it slower, the same voice bellowed, "You do not wish for to answer me? You dare? How are you called, you rude result of a triple-thumbed dwarf who raped his hunchbacked mother? I wish for to know how your name is spelled so that we can get it right on your tombstone!"

Longarm just kept riding. He flinched in his saddle but didn't duck when the loudmouth back on *El Camino Real* let fly a couple of six-gun rounds his way. There'd be time enough to go for his own side arm when and if he heard them chasing after him. It had sounded like two riders on their way to town together, from the hoofbeats he'd hoped to ride around, hoping they might not have heard his own, with the slight land breeze in his favor.

They didn't come after him. They fired no more shots.

90

It seemed likely at least one of them had the sense to warn his pal to cut it out. Pegging shots at folk you didn't know along *El Camino Real* after dark, could take years off a fool's life. For the highways betwixt towns were patrolled by *los rurales*, who shot first and asked questions afterwards, because *los rurales* were not out patrolling the highways and byways of rural Mexico after dark in search of lost children.

So when he heard another fusilade of pistol shots, further out of range, praise the Lord, Longarm reined his pinto to his left just in case as he muttered, "I wish they wouldn't let mean drunks tote guns down this way."

But no metal bees seemed to be buzzing out his way and as there came no more shots he figured the more sensible rider of the two had mentioned *los rurales* as well.

So he took his sweet time getting back to the post road. Then he went on his way, passed through a roadside cluster of *chozas* built of sticks and straw around a water pump, and swung inland at the next crossroad.

There was no official gate to the ranch, or *hacienda* in point of fact, since Don Hernan raised all sorts of things besides hell, because his dominion extended as far and included that water break he collected tribute on. But Longarm knew he was getting warmer when a trio of yard dogs commenced to serenade him by moonlight.

He didn't care. There were always yard dogs and in country where mean drunks toted guns, yard dogs were never allowed to run free. They were only meant to give the alarm as they lunged at the ends of their chains.

Longarm saw they had when a square of lamplight through an open door winked on up ahead. He reined in and called out, "*Ayudame, por favor! Estoy perdido.*"

He knew his lie had sold when a shemale voice invited him to come on in and have some tortillas and coffee whilst they set him straight on where he was and put him back on the right path to wherever he was headed.

A ragged-ass kid ran out to take the reins of his hired mount from him as Longarm got down in front of the long *ramada* running the length of the front of the rambling ranch house. The *chica* who'd come to the door barefoot with a horn lantern greeted him with a murmured assurance that her *patrona* had been expecting him.

She led him back through a well-appointed maze of rooms around a patio to what looked and smelled like the private chambers of a lady of quality. The plump little thing of some substantial means, if not a hell of a lot of quality, rose from the chaise she'd been lounging on with a box of chocolates to extend a soft hand as the *chica* backed out to leave them alone.

"I am called la Doña Inez," the butterball in old Spanish lace informed Longarm in passable English as he brushed the back of her wrist with his mustache.

She sat back down and patted a space beside her as she sweetly added, "I know for why you are here, of course. La Dama Tigra said she would send someone brave and determined. But I did not expect you to come here to our house for to kill my husband."

Chapter 11

So now Longarm knew who'd ordered the assassination of Don Hernan Yasquez Padilla and there went another grand notion. For how in God's green acres might you tell a man his wife's hired someone to kill him under the very same roof with said wife?

Remaining on his feet, Longarm kept a poker face and tried not to show much curiousity as he asked if the man of the house might be home.

Doña Inez inhaled another chocolate bonbon with a reproachful look up at him to sigh and say, "I told you he told me he had to attend a wedding reception in the town. He did not tell me he'd be stopping off at the palace of his *puta* before and after. But I knew that was for why he left here so early after sunset. He rode in with our *segundo*, young Miguel. He does not know I know Miguel holds his horse for him whenever he sees something he'd like to eat, drink or fuck. You just missed them. I am surprised you did not meet them on your way here."

Longarm said, "I think I did. I didn't know who they might be. So I rode around them, the more fool me. It's been grand talking to you, ma'am. But I'd better get cracking if I mean to catch up with them."

She patted the plush beside her again as she replied, "You do not wish for to take such a chance, now that you are safely inside this house. Young Miguel is a formidable fighter who drinks carefully and carries a big Schofield horse pistol. But Miguel will go to his own chambers when they ride back from town, and my husband will not have his own guns on when he staggers back to my bedchamber, for to fuck me with his fat, limp *piton* without even washing it off after all the places it will have been this night!"

Longarm cautiously remarked he could see how she might feel vexed with her man, but added, "My instructions were to pick a fight with him at that wedding shindig and blue-streak to a nearby hideout to lay low long enough for your authorities to decide it was a fair fight. Shooting a man under his own roof, in his own wife's bedchamber, can be sort of tough to explain in a courtroom."

She insisted, "Who is to ever know? These are my new orders. I wish for just this once to see the expression on his proud face when the shoe is on the other foot. I wish for him to find me in bed with another man. A younger man. A better-looking man. A man with hair on his chest and a gun under the pillow. Then I wish for to tell him you fuck better, whether you do or not, just before you kill him!"

Longarm whistled and said, "I take that back. You ain't vexed with Don Hernan, you're sore as hell at him! They told me he could be sort of hard to get along with."

"He has *shamed* me!" his plump little wife hissed in a voice dripping oil of vitriol. He didn't need every detail, but she insisted on running on about the way she'd been raised a decent convent gal, only to be wed to a monster who insisted on shoving it to her and the servants where no natural woman really enjoyed it.

She added, "For you I would gladly take it all three ways, if only for to tell him I had, willingly, just before you kill him! Come, let us repair to my *dormitorio* and get out of these warm clothes! We shall have plenty of time for to get to know one another better as we wait for that *pura mierda* they made me marry against my will!"

Longarm sicerely replied, "I thank you for such a tempting offer, ma'am. But the Tiger Lady wants me to pick a fight with him at that brawl in town. So that's where I aim to carry out my orders."

She wailed that she was paying for the services and hadn't enjoyed a good lay since before she'd been married. But Longarm kept going, got outside, gave that *muchacho* a *Yanqui* nickel for holding his pony so long, and mounted up to ride back to Matamoros, wondering how in blue thunder he'd ever cut Don Hernan out of the herd without hurting him, long enough to talk sense to him.

From what his plump, two-faced woman had just said, their *segundo* cum bodyguard was a rider of more common sense who stayed sober so's his boss could live through getting drunk and mean in an unhealthy clime for mean drunks. So did he play that card right, he and this Miguel, betwixt them, might get the condemned man out of there without a fight. Knowing he didn't really have much to come home to before he could shed a murderous spouse might make it easier for him to hide out until they could put that Tiger Lady out of business.

Down the road ahead he spotted torchlight and heard the low rumble of many voices. So he rode wide around what seemed a bunch of *vaqueros* gathering for a moonlight roundup, idly wondering what was up over yonder. Nothing else seemed to be going on, south of town. So he rode on in, returned his hired mount and its gear to the livery, and strode over to that wedding reception near the *Plaza de Toros*.

The party had gotten to the mellow stage and nobody paid a strange Anglo much mind as they stared at a familiar figure out in the middle of the dance floor, clapping their hands in time with the clatter of her heels as *La Gitana* from across the river, or a gypsy gal who worked as a whore across the river, performed a passable as well as noisy *flamenco*. A tired-looking old man against the wall behind her was baying like a she-coyote as he beat up his guitar with his knuckles. So Longarm was able to ask another gal clapping her hands nearby if his pal, Miguel, had ridden in with Don Hernan as yet.

The well-oiled and not bad *mestiza* said she hadn't seen either that night and suggested the two of them might be taking turns with that disgusting Consuela Lopez who thought she was so high and mighty.

He ducked back out before she could get a really good look at him. The address they'd given for that mistress, Consuela, was a short ride or a fair walk. It took him nigh twenty minutes and once he got there he saw no other way to go about it but to step up to the oaken door lit up by a hanging lantern in the middle of an otherwise blank stucco wall, and knock. There was no sign of Miguel or anybody else holding horses out front.

The door popped open at once, to reveal another vision in old Spanish lace, a lot younger and less well-fed, with her black hair unbound and an adoring look in her big brown eyes until she saw who she was staring up at. Then, in Spanish, she begged him to forgive her state of dress, explained she'd been getting ready for bed after waiting up a spell for somebody else, and asked if there was anything she could possibly do for him.

Longarm seriously doubted Don Hernan would cotton to him telling the pretty little thing what might be possible, seeing nobody else was there at the moment. But he told her he was a pal with a message for the one she'd been waiting up for. When she suggested he give it to her he said it was personal and asked when he might expect Don Hernan to come calling on her.

She told him in a puzzled tone that she'd expected her . . . protector earlier. He'd said he meant to take her to a *recepción*. She told him about that bullfighter getting hooked and suggested Don Hernan might have gone on without her. She looked away as she softly added he'd done things like that before. Don Hernan sounded like a swell guy, but it was still against the law to gun a man just for being a pissant.

Thanking the pretty little thing with a sincere smile, since it was easy to feel sorry for all of Don Hernan's womenfolk, Longarm said he'd try that reception and headed back toward the center of town, intending no such thing.

He'd visited all but one of the places listed on that note he had burned. He could truthfully say he hadn't been able to catch up with their chosen target at any of the places suggested. The last address was an ace in the hole he didn't need. You had no call to hide out when you hadn't done anything. So there was nothing to stop him from hopping the ferry across to Brownsville and reporting an honest try to Tom Corrigan.

Nothing except all those waving torches over all those big gray someros gathered on the ferry landing. Longarm didn't feel like asking excited *rurales* what they were so excited about at this hour. So he faded back the way he'd come and ducked into the first open doorway he came to.

He found himself in an old Spanish church with coral-block walls and live-oak timbers, dimly lit by votive candles in ruby-glass *tazas* and smelling of a hundred years worth of incense and honest sweat.

Longarm slipped into a pew to gather his wits. He hadn't done anything. So they couldn't be after him, as Mormon Mike Mason. But on the other hand, *La Gitana* couldn't be the only Mexican down this way who'd ever heard of *El Brazo Largo* and there was still that bounty on the head of such a *Yanqui muy malo*.

"Don't be so modest," he muttered to himself. "You can't be the only one *los rurales* would be after and that border crossing is the natural place to head anybody off."

He sat there muttering to himself about the pros and cons as, sweeping up near the altar, a motherly nun took his mutterings for anguished prayers. She left him be for quite a spell. Then she timidly came back to ask him if he'd like her to fetch the *padre* for him.

He rose, shaking his head, but thanking her for the thought. He made sure she saw him dropping something in their poor box on his way out. They'd just earned it. He had his wits back together, now.

When he risked a peek around a distant corner he saw they still had the ferry landing covered. So he headed next for that last address on the list he'd committed to memory.

The lettering on the window glass never mentioned La Dama Tigra. It only promised to advise you on family, financial and romantic matters with the help of cards or the lines of your own palm. At that hour, in Mexico, the place was still open for business. So Longarm went on in to find himself alone, for the moment, near a bitty round table set up with two chairs in front of heavy red and black brocaded drapes.

Then a pale, well-manicured hand poked out through a slit in the drapes to beckon him deeper into the spooky interior as a sultry she-male voice asked in English,

"What kept you so long? I've been expecting you for hours!"

As he joined a gal in gypsy dress with mighty odd hair in an even more spooky back room, she trilled up at him, "Word of your success has proceeded you. But what on earth were you doing out on the streets after stirring up such a hornet's nest?"

He said he'd been to church as he sized her up whilst trying not to say anything he couldn't take back. He could see why they called her a tiger lady. She was of pure Spanish or mayhaps any brand of European blood, despite her gypsy skirts and off-the-shoulder cotton blouse. He'd seen black-headed gals with streaks of blond in their hair and he'd seen blond gals with darker streaks. But this one had to dye her hair, if it was real, to manage such an even distribution of blond and brunette cascading down about her oval face to frame those big green eyes. He could see she touched up the corners of those feline eyes with mascara. No white woman came with eyes that slanty. It wasn't too clear whether she was shooting for desirable or spooky. She looked both and it was tough not to wonder what it might be like to strip her bare ass, provided with a chair and whip.

The Tiger Lady led him from her inner sanctum provided with skull candlesticks and more disturbing sights to a regular Mex kitchen with a corner cooking-hearth and a plank table painted the usual shade of indigo blue. There was this Mex notion that flies hated the color. It might have been true. Longarm had never taken the time to count flies on many Mex tables of any color.

The Tiger Lady sat him down and rustled up some Arbuckle coffee and store-bought marble cake instead of the usual tortillas. When Longarm told her he didn't take coffee, and that hurt like fire, she fetched him some hot chocolate, purring, "I'd forgotten you Mormons don't sin with coffee, tobacco or demon rum. You're not going to

99

get anything extra for gunning that segundo, you know. The deal we agreed to called for you to take care of Don Hernan and Don Hernan alone, remember?"

Longarm didn't answer, having no idea what he was supposed to say.

She sat down across from him, patted the back of his wrist, and told him, "Don't pout. We'll try to make it up to you. But there's only so much to go around."

He bit into some marble cake and washed it down with the chocolate, a Mexican invention they even spread on chickens if you didn't stop them, and muttered something about wanting to be fair to everybody.

She beamed across the table at him, saying, "I was hoping you'd be all they promised and, my God, you must have nerves of steel! You're not even breathing hard as you sit there with a hundred guns trying to cut your trail outside."

Longarm shrugged, had some more cake, and dryly asked why anyone would want to cut the trail of a Latter Day Saint just visiting Old Mexico in hope of making some converts to the Salt Lake Temple.

She laughed, dirty, and purred, "Why indeed? You were seen at that reception, looking for your man. His mistress recalls you coming to her very door in search of him before you headed right out to his hacienda, bold as Daniel striding into the lion's den, to gun him along with his segundo and bodyguard as they were riding into town, you *lobo muy furioso!*"

"If you say so." Longarm shrugged cautiously, as he tried to fathom where she'd ever come up with such a notion.

She said, "You are safe here, with me. They will still be watching the ferry for days or more. But *mañana*, when things calm down a little, I will show you my own private means of crossing the Rio Bravo, up a little ways, where other *asociados* dwell amid the willows and sometimes go fishing in this old log *piragua*, no?"

He said he'd go along with any suggestions she had to make, adding, "I take it you do business, all sorts of business, on both sides of the border?"

She replied without hesitation or shame, "A woman alone does what she must to get by in this man's world. *Yanqui* clients on the *Tejano* side of the Rio Bravo naturally have more to spend. On the other hand, more people down this way seem to have someone they wish for to see dead. So it, how you say, evens out?"

He said that sounded about the way he'd put it. He asked how many late night clients or household help they had to worry about.

She said, "I was just about to close for the night. As I told you out front, I expected you some time ago. Is almost midnight and cool enough for to sleep, at last. Would you like to go to bed with me, now?"

He knew he didn't have much time to decide on his answer. Since Hell had no fury, but defense lawyers could be such pains in the ass when the arresting officer had been compromised by the accused or his own weak nature.

He knew that she knew that as well as any other crook of the unfair sex. So, seeing this could be a test, and it wasn't a federal offense to screw any lady in Old Mexico, Longarm told the Tiger Lady he'd be proud to go to bed with her.

Chapter 12

Her parlor floor above the shop was furnished more in the current fashions, albeit a tad flashy, as you'd expect from a lady who'd grown up with less money to spend on frills than she'd been pulling in more recent.

Her bed was a four-poster carved naughty with cherubs playing grab-ass up and down all four posts and across the headboard. The bedstead was naturally hung with mosquito netting and nobody used quilts in high summer down this way. So he could see right off how her sheets and all six pillowcases were shiny satin printed in black and yaller to look like slippery tiger skins. The Tiger Lady undressed bold as brass in front of him by lamplight. So he proceeded to do the same, only mildly disappointed to discover her pubic hair was neither blond nor brunette. She'd shaved her old ring-dang-doo bare as a baby's behind.

He consoled himself that at least he wouldn't have to worry about crabs. She beat him into bed, of course, and her first indication of shyness came when she stared at what he had rising to the occasion to marvel, "Belle might have warned me! She said you were great in bed, but she never mentioned you aiming a weapon of that caliber at her!"

Longarm suspected she was flattering him. It seemed it was always the bold and brassy ones with knowing eyes who brought up the dimensions of his manhood. Longarm had never inspired enough erections from other men to be an expert on such matters. But he knew heaps of men worried about being big enough. So whores tended to tell anyone with a pecker bigger than a peanut what a scary stud he was.

He was more certain he was being tested when they got right down to cases and he began to wish he had that chair and whip. Once she'd come ahead of him—more than once, she said—she offered further favors he knew few women enjoyed as much as men, simply because that was the ways men and women were designed by Mother Nature.

When he told her he was an old-fashioned boy who liked it just as well where he had it in her, the Tiger Lady started to act as if she might be getting sort of fond of him. It made him feel like a shit.

He knew that did he arrest her on the Texican side of the border her lawyer couldn't make much of him screwing her in Mexico, off-duty. She and her pals weren't the only ones who could slip across borders to their own advantage. So, shitty as it might make him, he just had to get her to carry him back to Texas and . . . then what?

Whether Don Hernan and his *segundo* were really dead or not, south of the border, neither the State of Texas nor the Union Longarm rode for had any juristiction over a treacherous wife or the assassination contractor she'd turned to with her troubles. Longarm knew that even if he could establish a Brownsville residency or American citizenship for any of the bunch they'd never in this world spend a night in jail for anything he could prove in court.

He was really out of sorts with the Book of Mormon once they'd paused for breath and some pillow talk. He was used to smoking in bed with a pal at such times. Passing a cheroot back and forth gave a man time to weigh his words in the company of a wicked woman who might be out to trip him up.

But there were advantages to keeping his mouth shut with a friendly hand in her lap. For, being a woman, however wicked, she had a time keeping still when there was another human ear within a furlong.

Her lewd remark about his old organ grinder had already confirmed his suspicion that she'd ordered Madame Belle to bed down with him for some questions and answers, bless both their soft hides, and he hoped old Belle had enjoyed herself, too. So whether this one was the real boss of the operation or not, she had to be higher on the totem pole as well as south of the border. He was now about convinced it was a Tex-Mex gang astraddle the border so's the big guns could jump either way. It was easy to see why. They were playing for high stakes with their necks against the law, with blood money sweetening the pot for them. He knew better than to ask her how much they'd charged Doña Inez. She volunteered the dribs and drabs of information off the street she had used to put the picture together all wrong.

She had the timing wrong, to begin with. Nobody had offered her any exact chronology as they'd placed Mormon Mike or someone who looked like him at that reception, the lamplit doorway of Consuela Lopez or out at the victim's own private home, like a *tiburón* scenting blood in the water. So she'd naturally placed him wherever he worked best in sequence, up to where he must have caught up with the *ranchero* and his *segundo* on *El Camino Real* and shot it out with the both of them.

Forking a long, shapely leg across him by lamplight leaving nothing about her to his imagination, the Tiger Lady reached down between them to work it up for the both of them as she told him how others riding into town had found the two bodies sprawled in the moonlit road and alerted *los rurales*. By torchlight the Mex lawmen had determined Don Hernan's bodyguard had been gutshot thrice, point-blank, while the intended victim, Vasquez, had been hit in the back of the skull to have most of his face blown off as he'd obviously tried to get away.

Lowering her pulsating ring-dang-doo to envelope his throbbing organ grinder, the dragon lady purred, "I can picture it as if I was there! For all his bluster Don Hernan tried to hide behind his underling, Miguelito. Is this reward enough for the way you stood up to a gunfighter in his own right, *querido mio*?"

He allowed it was way easier on his nerves and rolled her on her back to do her right with an elbow hooked under either of her widespread knees as she bit down on the back strokes and opened wide to say "ah" as he drove it to the roots the other way.

He had things pictured another way. Albeit he never said so as he pounded her to glory. Since he, himself, had been nowhere near either of them, he suspected the testy Don Hernan had lost his temper with a *segundo* telling him he was behaving like an asshole, blew poor old Miguel out of his saddle, gut shot, and caught a lucky round from a dying man on the ground as he'd tried to ride on. But as that comical vaudville gal had told him one time on Larimer Street, whenever your audience applauds the wrong line it's smarter to take a bow and let on that was what you meant all the time.

Once they were doing it in the more conversational

dog-style he made up a few details about the bother it had been to catch up with Don Hernan and his body-guard, larded on how the cowardly cuss had screamed and tried to get away, lest his wife doubt she'd gotten her money's worth, and allowed he was sorry for not following instructions to the letter.

He said, "Sometimes, when a man won't stand and fight as you were banking on, you have to sort of impro-vise."

She arched her back to purr, "I read in that newspaper how you shot that private investigator at his desk at clos-ing time. How did you get them to suspect it was that dentist?"

Longarm thrust deep to modestly admit, "Just lucky, I reckon. I'd like to be able to say I planned things that way. But to tell the pure truth I didn't know the wife-cheater. I just hoped that, seeing old Eagle Emerson had so many others he was investigating, they might let me ride off betwixt the raindrops."

She asked just what they'd been trying to pin on him up to Del Rio, since the modest bounty fliers had only allowed he was wanted by them for questioning.

He thrust hard enough to hit bottom and make her wince as he asked, "How come you all keep pestering me about what they might want me for up the border a ways? Don't you have enough on me, as of this very evening, down this way?"

She laughed, dirty, arched her spine as if she liked him hitting bottom and confided, "I've been wondering how to stress that point without it sounding like a threat. Now that you've carried out your first job as directed, none of us are in any position to play one another false. We know we can trust one another and that's the best way for this game to be played. *No crées*?"

He agreed that was about the size of it as he kept it to

106

himself that he'd cut another sign. The Tiger Lady lived in Mexico, wore Mex duds and went out of her way to sound Mex. But he suspected it was as likely she was a natural blonde streaking her hair with black dye. He knew he could never hope to pass for Mex, up close, with his limited grasp of the lingo and Mex ways. But, good as the Tiger Lady was with the lingo and no doubt Mexican marriage problems, he detected just a hint of Dixie Drawl in her fake Mex accent. He had to take anything she said in Spanish at face value. He knew just enough of the lingo to sense she was trying to sound sort of Spanish Gypsy, from the old country, when she sort of lisped some words. A Mex born in Mexico pronounced their word for blue, *azul*, about the way it was spelled, *"Ah-sool."* A gypsy lady raised in Old Spain, and likely knowing way more ancient spells than your average *bruja mestiza* or half-breed witch, would pronounce *azul "Ah-thool"* the way this one did. But there was no getting around that aftertaste of gumbo in her broken English and Madame Belle Lasalle was no-bones-about-it Creole, too.

He thought about that as they wound up cuddled against the tiger-striped pillow piled under that cherub orgy across the head of her bed. They hinted more at the French Quarter of New Orleans than the original Southern stock who'd migrated west to Texas back in the early twenties. Accents were funny things. English-speaking folk all across their new world from Canada to the Mex borders had evolved different accents that sounded nothing like the different ways folk spoke English back in the British Isles. He suspected all regional accents evolved, to use Professor Darwin's term, because the kids of a mom raised with one accent and a dad raised with another wound up talking a mixture that was neither one or the other when you got to listening tight. A schoolmarm he knew with grand legs and an interest in his own West-By-God-Virginia accent had told him the professors held that New England Yankee had commenced as a mixture of regional accents from the *south* of England whilst the Dixie way of talking had come down from settlers from the *north* of England, with the mountain folk along the Appalachians influenced by Scotch-Irish that has been passed through the earlier northern and southern English along the Atlantic tidewater and piedmont. So when you listened tight to the Tiger Lady, her broken English didn't work. She'd been raised in some household where educated Spanish and Delta Dixie had been spoken, he felt surer, every time they swapped more spit and she told him how proud she was to be working with him.

When he asked if she was talking about working with him in or out of bed she laughed and said she didn't find what they'd been doing in bed anything but pleasure.

She added, "We have lost some of our best gunfighters, just as our business has been picking up. A professional picker of quarrels, almost as good as you, was arrested before he could finish the job we sent him for to do, in Colorado. As we feared, a most dangerous lawman they called Longarm somehow got something out of him. We lost another good *pistolero* for certain and perhaps another was hurt, or frightened into early retirement, when they shot it out with this Longarm in a place called Parsons Junction."

Longarm kneaded a nipple thoughtfully as he told her Tom Corrigan had mentioned something about that. He said, "They managed to gun the famous Longarm as well, right?"

She said, "*Es verdad.* But Bunny Weed has failed to return and would not be wise for to send Juan Pablo

Jones to Denver for to finish a job began by . . . well, a gringo, meaning no disrespect."

He lightly replied, "None taken. Like I told this old Lakota who asked if I minded being called a *Wasichu*, you don't insult a white man by calling him anything but late for breakfast. You have to feel sort of delicate about what you are before it hurts you to be so designated. Words such as Dago, Wop and such might make some immigrants wince a might. Call a man a Yankee, a Reb or Limey and he just sticks his chest out further."

She asked, "When were you called a *Wasichu* by some Sioux? I was told you were from Utah Territory?"

Kicking himself mental for the slip, Longarm cum Mormon Mike just chuckled fondly and said, "Digging irrigation channels along the aprons of those infernal Wasach mountains until I never wanted to see Utah with its pesky Shoshoni or Paiutes again. I made friends with some Sioux—they call themselves Lakota—running guns and firewater to them up along the Bozeman Trail. Nobody never made a dime running guns and firewater to *Paiute*. The poor ragged rascals can't pay in anything but pine nuts and rabbit hides!"

He knew it had worked when she changed the subject in a bored tone, saying, "I'm sorry I asked. We were talking about that job Solitaire Stryker had been sent up to Denver to perform for . . . a certain client of ours."

"What's in it for me?" asked Longarm as Mormon Mike.

She said, "Not so fast, *mi corazón*. The . . . matter is being, how you say, renegotiated?"

He replied, "That's about what I'd settle for if I sent one old boy to gun somebody and he got picked up by the law. What's holding up the show? Has your client suffered a change of heart?"

She answered, simply, "Is more like a bout of nerves.

As I said, the one we sent to Denver for to do the job was picked up on older charges before he could get, how you say, set up? Poor Solitaire had not been given his final instructions. So he will not betray our most nervous client. But he must have told the one called Longarm about his boardinghouse in Brownsville."

Longarm as Mormon Mike nibbled her ear and mused, "I can see why you sent them gents to Parsons Junction. You have other pals in Denver, eh?"

She sighed and said, "One needs all the friends one can get, in this business. We were hoping that, as we had been told, this Longarm might be playing the lone wolf. If he had told his own friends about Madame Belle's they would have sent someone else, by now."

"That's how come Tom Corrigan was so suspicious when I showed up," mused Longarm. That had been a statement, not a question.

She answered it as a question anyway, saying, "*Si*, we were divided whether to recruit you or poison you. We had planned for to send Juan Pablo Jones after Don Hernan Vasquez Padilla."

He chuckled into her ear and said, "I sort of wondered if you all were testing me. No lawman would have done the deed for you, right?"

She replied without shame, "He would have given some lame excuse, and then, of course, we would have made certain he never left *La Boca del Rio Bravo* alive."

Chapter 13

They rose late the next morning for more reasons than one. They both needed the rest, she wasn't open for business before late in the day and it seemed earlier out than it really was.

The day had dawned overcast as winds from the gulf threatened more summer rain and cooled things down considerably. It happened along the Gulf Coast on occasion. So they tore off a morning quickie and then she served him breakfast in bed.

She was working too hard on her Mex accent to rustle up any gumbo. But the usual *huevos rancheros con tortillas* was an acquired taste as well, and it seemed she did business with more Mexicans than she served breakfast in bed to. So he had to settle for plain bacon and eggs.

It made a man feel special.

The cooler but threatening weather had her worried about crossing the river upstream in a dug-out canoe. So once they'd bathed and dressed she told him to sit tight and slipped out for some scouting, locking up behind her.

Longarm took adavantage of being left alone in her

quarters in a sort of rude fashion, reflecting that he didn't need a Mexican search warrant because he didn't ride for Mexico.

But he failed to find any written records of any description, save for rent slips made out to a Sra. Martinez. She had a whole mess of books devoted to odd notions, from Atlantis to Voodoo, in English as well as Spanish. He found a Spanish edition of *The Prince* by Mister Machiavelli, banned in Spain by King Phillip and in England by Queen Elizabeth for identical reasons. *The Prince* explained how politics really worked and what kindly princes and potentates pulled on the public on the sneak. Longarm saw she hadn't bothered to pick up a copy of that other book poor Mister Machiavelli had writ about the advantages of democracy under a republic. Hardly anyone remembered he'd been trying to show both sides of the question, reporting in *The Prince* how one-man rule only worked when that one man was a total bastard. It was a caution how many scoundrels since had decided *The Prince* was a self-help book.

Some of her other tomes on Tarot cards and such were just silly and there was a book on gypsy tea-leaf reading that reminded him of that scene in Mister Victor Hugo's novel where the Gypsy gal, Esmeralda, defends herself from a witchcraft charge by demanding to know how come her folk live from pillar to post in rags, telling fortunes for pennies, if they possess a possible lick of secret power.

He didn't waste time reading any of her occult crap and since any real Mormon Mike wouldn't smoke, he got to pace the floor above her shop a lot before she slipped back inside, laughing.

She told him *los rurales* weren't watching the ferry crossing, now, and suggested just before *la siesta*, when folk would be crowding on board lest they wind up stuck

112

on the wrong side of the border with nothing to do, would be safe enough for him to cross.

She said some Mex police detective had added things up all wrong and decided Don Hernan, known to be a mean drunk, had gut-shot his *segundo*, known to be good with a gun, to be shot in return by the dying Miguel before he rode on. When she marveled how anyone could have imagined such an unlikely scene, Longarm felt no call to point out how differing diameters and angles of bullet wounds might be read by a lawman who knew his onions. It seemed a shame *El Presidente* had anyone that good on his payroll.

But Longarm wasn't about to argue and so, taking advantage of that dumb detective, he parted company from the Tiger Lady with a wistful kiss, once she'd told him, sad-eyed, how unlikely it seemed they'd be getting together again in the near future. She told him to go back to that boardinghouse and wait for further instructions. He'd already noticed that no matter who was really in charge, nobody seemed to give direct orders you could nail them for in a U.S. court of law.

The sky was still overcast and threatening rain as he boarded the ferry, unchallenged, for the short crossing back to Brownsville. When he sought a windward place to enjoy the unseasonable breeze, he found himself at the starboard rail with that gypsy whore, *La Gitana*.

She waited for him to speak first. Nobody else being within earshot, he told her she'd done a fine job of rumor-mongering about Mormon Mike and added, "I saw you at that reception last night. You dance swell."

She shrugged and said, "*Gracias*. Was only for, how you say, fun? I return to my country for to enjoy myself. I got back to your country for to make a living."

He didn't ask why she didn't try to make it in show business as a dancer. Other gals who had had told him

113

how they'd gotten screwed but a tad less often for less money in the end.

He said, "I met up with that La Dama Tigra last night. She intimated she was a gypsy, I mean a *gitana*, as well."

La Gitana, who's professional name indicated she was a member of a rare breed in Matamoros, sniffed and said, "Does not matter what you people call us. Among ourselves we are *Romana* and La Dama Tigra is not Romana. I do not believe that hair, either."

Longarm didn't tell her how he'd come to the conclusion, but told her, "If it's a wig it's a good one that she's pinned down tight. How can you be so certain she ain't one of you Roman folk? Do you know her all that well?"

La Gitana shook her own wild mane of unkept blackness to reply, "I have never spoke to her. But I have seen her, on both sides of this river and . . . We know one another on sight. Do not ask me how. I do not know how men who like boys seldom approach the wrong boys, either."

He allowed he followed her drift. He knew Indians and colored folk were good at spotting distant cousins passing for white, unchallenged by most white folk. He hadn't thought that Tiger Lady had been a gypsy to begin with and it was interesting to learn she sometimes came over to Uncle Sam's jurisdiction in her mysterious travels.

When their ferry nosed into the Brownsville landing, *La Gitana* asked if he'd care for a quick suck, or even a fuck, before she got down to business in the land of opportunity.

Not wanting to hurt her feelings needlessly, he told her truthfully that he'd just come in another gal and added, gallantly, he regretted his inability to take her up on such a generous offer.

So *La Gitana* strutted up the quay with her spirits lifted

114

and Longarm, as Mormon Mike, went back to the nearby boardinghouse.

Tom Corrigan was seated out front on the steps, enjoying another swell cigar, damn it, as Longarm joined him there to say no more than "Howdy. Looks like rain" as he waited to see what happened next.

The older man in rumpled white linen took the tempting smoke from his lips to quietly say, "We heard. You must have more balls than the marbles champ at my old reform school. What ever possessed you to go after your man most every damn place he could have been, last night?"

Longarm, as Mormon Mike, shrugged and modestly replied, "You ordered me to gun him. I had to find him, first."

Corrigan said, "Hold on, now, Mormon Mike. I'll thank you to recall you never got any such orders from *me,* personal. I told you somebody I knew wanted somebody taken care of. I told you you'd get more detailed instructions at that *Cantina del Camino Real.*"

Longarm snorted, "Aw, shit, why are we still acting coy as pimple-faced kids at our first grange dance? Are you afraid I'll stand before a judge and admit I shot two men last night because you asked me to?"

Corrigan dryly remarked, "I wasn't there, your honor. All I know is what I read in the papers."

Longarm, as Mormon Mike, asked what was supposed to happen next. The older fellow boarder, as far as he could prove, shrugged and told him, "If I was you I'd go up to my room and open any envelope I found on my bed. I wouldn't ask Madame Belle or any of her help how it got there or what might be in it. They won't be able to tell you and such questions just upset them."

Longarm nodded, went on in, and mounted the steps to unlock the door of his hired room with his own key.

115

He saw they'd wedged the match stem back upside down again. He liked to wedge one head first into the bottom hinge because he'd noticed most folk thought it best to have the head of a match sticking out.

The envelope on his pillow contained another two hundred and fifty dollars in paper, with a terse note informing him he was free to head on out to sea or await further instructions. So he left with close to a year's salary for an honest workingman burning a hole in his pocket.

He would have given some to *La Gitana* for a service rendered, had he spotted her anywhere along the quay. But it seemed her other business had picked up with the overcast day so reasonable for fornication with *la siesta* in full progress, now, for more traditional border folk.

You found things open and shut, helter-skelter, in a Tex-Mex border town during the siesta hours betwixt noon and four P.M. regardless of the weather outside. So he managed to order a T-bone smothered in chili at a half-deserted beanery, dying for the black coffee Mormon Mike would be unlikely to order, and then, seeing he'd likely be stuck in Brownsville a spell, as that client in the market for a Denver killing made up his or her mind, he ambled over to the bookstore Velma Oakhurst worked in, to see how she felt about a set-down Chinese supper that evening.

He found the well-built mousy-headed Velma alone and looking bored as she swept new and used volumes with a turkey-feather duster. She seemed delighted to have company, but when he asked her whether they had a supper engagement or not she glanced at the Monitor Brand clock on the far wall to allow it was too early to tell. She said she'd just had dinner at Madame Belle's and wasn't sure what she'd feel like having for supper, once she recovered from half-incinerated red snapper

116

with what had seemed fried green pepper filled with snail slime.

Longarm chuckled and allowed she was talking about fried okra, an acquired taste as could make a man grateful he'd missed out on noon dinner at their boardinghouse and had had to settle for steak, instead.

But despite his light banter, Longarm was running out of patience with a mousy-haired miss who didn't look easy, before she commenced to bob and weave.

He allowed he'd poke about amongst the stacks in hopes of finding something else to occupy his mind, later on that evening. If she took that as a hint, she might be spurred to make up her skittish mind. If she was too dumb to see he was about ready to give up, it would be a heaps smarter to give up in *poco tiempo*, before he'd spent any money on her.

There was more to the bookstore than met the eye, coming in. He found a washroom and a back door behind a screening floor-to-ceiling wall of children's books, new and used. He had no call to piss. But he tried the back door to find it locked and, having no use for anything by the Brothers Grimm or Mister Lewis Carroll, he was about to wander on back in sight from the front when he heard the bell over the street door tinkle and decided to stay put, lest anyone wonder why a gent in blue denims and a .44-40 was keeping company with a bookstore gal.

He pretended to read a used copy of *Black Beauty*, about the dumbest book about horses ever written, as he listened to Velma wait on some gent with no hesitation in her voice at all.

Of course, all that male customer wanted was that new book about Ben Hur in the olden days of the Holy Land. It took Velma no time at all to send him on his way and ring the sale up. So Longarm was about to rejoin her, and invite her, firmly, one last time, when the door chime warned of another customer and so, not wanting a show-down with the mouse-haired gal in front of witnesses, Longarm stayed put.

Then he blinked in surprise as a familiar voice, albeit missing its Mex accent, asked Velma if they had that book she'd ordered yet.

Longarm gingerly removed a volume at eye level to peek through the stacked books to make sure and, sure enough, there stood the Tiger Lady, albiet dressed like an Anglo lady of some means and he'd been right about her professional hairdo. Without that cleverly pinned-on wig, the Tiger Lady was a way more refined looking beauty with chestnut curls and way less makeup, if she was wearing any at all. When gals really knew how to make themselves up, a mere man couldn't tell.

Velma told whoever in hell that was out yonder that they were still waiting for her theosophy tomes and she left, trying to sound nice to the younger gal.

When Longarm came back into view, Velma said, "Oh, there you are. What were you doing back there so quiet, Mister Mason? Were you hiding from Miss Martin for some reason?"

He answered, truthfully enough when you studied on it, "I've yet to meet a Miss *Martin* in these parts. Might she be someone I might want to avoid for some reason?"

Velma made a wry face and decided, "She's all right, I suppose. Just a little . . . peculiar."

Longarm tried not to sound interested as he casually replied, "I did notice she'd ordered some sort of peculiar reading material. I ain't certain what *theosophy* means, but it sounds mighty serious."

The girl who sold books for a living explained, "The theosophy or science of gods, plural, was started in Russia by an odder woman who calls herself Madame Bla-vatsky, Helena Patrovna Blavatsky, and some say she's

118

lying about that. Her occult movement is a mish-mash of witchcraft, fortune-telling, faith healing and you-name-it. For a nominal fee Madame Blavatsky's disciples will introduce you to a troll-king or the fairies in the bottom of your garden!"

Longarm tried not to sound too interested as he asked Velma if Miss Martin was a disciple of the theosophist movement.

Velma said, "Oh, heavens, no! Poor Cora Martin is just a bored and lonely widow with time on her hands and the wherewithall to indulge in the occult raving of Blavatsky, Churchward and De Sade. I doubt she has the education to grasp their full meanings, if any of those discredited but awfully expensive books have any meaning at all, to anyone with common sense. I'm paid to sell books. So sell them I must. But I wish I could tell the poor dear how she's just wasting her money."

Longarm suggested Cora Martin, as she was known on this side of the border, might feel she was getting some good out of all that razzle dazzle about magical powers. It would have been dumb to confide about rent slips made out to a Señora Martinez in Matamoros to a gal staying at the same boardinghouse and, in any case, he could always get the Brownsville address of Miss Cora Martin from their city directory.

Chapter 14

Now that he had other fish to fry and wasn't all that interested in having supper with her, Velma Oakhurst naturally decide she fancied Chinese food in the cool of the evening and asked whether he wanted to pick her up there at quitting time or leave from the boardinghouse at a more fashionable hour.

He suggested they might like to wash up and tell Madame Belle not to set out suppers for them. He didn't tell her he wanted to check the pillow in his own room for mail.

They agreed he'd be back around quitting time to walk her home. Then he got out of there, his mind in a whirl, as he tried to decide whether he ought to hold 'em or fold 'em.

As he headed for the civic center, knowing the way of old, Longarm weighed the odds and they read both ways. This practicing stage magician who liked to get on top had once explained spooky impossible coincidence to him. Everybody had to have an occasional dream come true or run into someone they hadn't thought about for years, just as they'd been thinking about 'em, because there were so blamed many of us.

With millions of folk having dream after dream, night after night, the odds were just impossible that nobody, nowhere, would have a dream that failed to come true. Nobody ever asked why the thousands of *other* dreams they had failed to pan out. Everybody thought constantly about everything and everybody as they poked about day by day. So, once again the odds on never bumping into anyone you were thinking about were just impossible and only spooky when you never considered how seldom such a thing happened. But, just the same, what were the odds on a gal he'd spent the night with in Mexico turning up in a bookstore north of the border as he was flirting with another gal entire?

But if she'd been following him, he decided as he strode along, she had to be dumb as a shingle. Could anybody think he was too dumb to see through a change in accent and hairdo after having his way with a gal, more ways than one, by lamplight?

It would have made way more sense to have some face he didn't know follow him, if they wanted him followed. He didn't know all the faces in their gang, despite those he'd met up with or eliminated so far.

Spotting another bookstore on the far side of the street, he crossed over to ask if they carried books on Lost Atlantis, Black Magic, White Magic or Voodoo. They told him to try the one where Velma Oakhurst worked. So, all right, a professional spook looking for some professional patter would have been steered poor Velma's way by other merchants or, seeing she boarded amid pals of the Tiger Lady, one of the same might have snooped around her bookstore, discovered volumes of interest to a fake gypsy fortune-teller and after that it worked as coincidence. A two-faced woman looking for odd reading material made more sense than a stupid move back yonder.

As he crossed the courthouse square toward the hall of records, in a beeline because he didn't have to cling to the afternoon shade in such an overcast day, Longarm strode the width of a football field in the open. So the man tailing him, not knowing just where they were headed, had to do the same and, even though he held well back, Longarm spotted him.

But as in the case of the other members of the gang he could point out in a court of law, the tall deputy didn't have anything on a one of them that he could prove, as yet. So he just kept going and when he got to the hall of records in the basement of the county courthouse the short, dark figure under a white planter's hat naturally waited outside.

Longarm didn't have time to weave fancies, so he took a chance and flashed his badge at the buck-toothed young gal presiding over the files and asked if he could have a peek at their city directory for openers.

She was too young and green to demand further identification, or mayhaps she didn't care because the city directory was meant to be read by most anybody.

Longarm didn't write down the address when he saw they did indeeed have a Mrs. Cora Martin down as a property owner and, better yet, said she was part-owner of a fashionable tearoom there in Brownsville and the owner in full of a boardinghouse managed by a Madame Belle Lasalle.

"This is commencing to read like incest," Longarm muttered to himself as he thanked the teenaged clerk and waited until he was out in the hall to hide his badge in the lining of one boot, again.

Then he found a stairwell and moved up a level to exit by way of a side door to the county courthouse, on the far side.

He scooted across to the shadows of some old Spanish

arches along the fronts of some shops facing anyone crossing the empty side street after him. But there seemed to be no takers. His secret admirer seemed to be expecting him to come out of that courthouse the same way he'd gone in.

Longarm felt a wry sympathy for the cuss, knowing how he had to be feeling at the moment. After riding for the Justice Department six or eight years, Longarm had been in the same fix, more than once, tailing a suspect alone. There was just no way to cover all the ways in and out of a building when your quarry ducked into one. If you ran around to the back he was just as likely to come back out the front. So you had to sit tight and hope for the best.

Longarm was glad he had somebody other than the Tiger Lady keeping tabs on him. It meant she hadn't known he was in the back when she'd dropped by to see about that occult book. He idly toyed with the notion of doubling around to tap his little shadow in the back and advise him that white planter's hat was a bad move. But then what? Mormon Mike, as Longarm had made him up, would never buy the cuss a drink. A real cold-blooded gun-for-hire would be more inclined to shoot first and consider headgear later.

So Longarm ambled on downstream to where the coastal vessels and clipper ships put in, admiring the forest of masts as he dallied amid the confusion of the broad cobblestone *embarcadero* and idly wondering how come, like the lonely whistle of a train passing by in the distance late at night, the sight of a clipper ship's bowsprit looming over you as you admired it from the cobblestones, planted safely ashore, made the kid in you hanker to sign aboard and run off to strange-sounding places beyond the far horizon.

He knew, from reading books near payday when his

drinking funds ran low, how awful some of those distant places ruled by mandarins, mikados and such could get. Once upon a time he'd been lured from his childhood by the haunting call of fifes and drums, to a strange-sounding place they called Shiloh. But there was likely something way back in the nooks and crannies of the human brain that pined for whatever in thunder lay over the far horizon, up under a strange skirt, or in the next hand you might be dealt, playing poker with a stranger called Doc. It was like that Professor Darwin suggested, the human race would have stayed up in the trees with the sensible apes if it hadn't been more curious about its surroundings.

He didn't ask anybody for a job aboard any of the vessels in port. He knew somebody would be more likely to remember a stranger wasting their time that way than a stranger they were too busy to look at. He knew anybody watching from a distance might buy his story that he was interested in leaving Texas by sea.

He knew he'd have to leave soon, one way or another, whether or not he was able to make any arrests. That Mex detective had put the death of Don Hernan Vasquez Padilla together right as rain. It was only a question of time before others wondered some about the derring-do of Mormon Mike and, even if they went on buying his wild tale, he was too well-known as an Anglo lawman wanted by Mex lawmen to risk much more time along the damned border. *La Gitana* had already spotted him, by shithouse luck in passing. How long might he have before it got around that, whether *El Brazo Largo* had been killed in Parsons Junction or not, someone who sure looked like him was in Brownsville?

He got back to the boardinghouse early and read one of those books in his hired room for a spell, the weather outside threatening more rain but making for comfort indoors.

Then it was going on quitting time. So he tossed aside the book to change into a fresh shirt, run a razor over his stubble, and head on back to the bookstore, smelling more of bay rum than armpit.

He found the mousy-haired Velma raring to go. He could smell she'd been at work in the washroom behind those kid books. When she told him she'd decided it might be best to just go on to that Chinese place, without going home first, he was willing.

She'd naturally closed up close to sundown. So even though it was still light out as they got to the chop suey joint on the quay, it was getting dark and the streetlamps were casting puddles of light on the cobblestones by the time they'd finished what she'd seemed to enjoy as a whole new experience. She was the only one who got to sip tea as they lingered by candlelight, of course. As Mormon Mike, Longarm really wanted some of that Chinee tea. It smelled swell and he knew nobody made tea better than Irish women and Chinese short-order cooks. But he had to act like a Latter Day Saint whose only vices were murder and fornication. So he complimented her on her taste for new experiences, resisted the offer to introduce her to some unusual positions from the *Kama Sutra* they sold under the counter at novelty shops and asked if that was what had lured a Penn State gal so far from home.

She sighed, sipped some more tea, and confessed she'd come to Texas to seek her fortune and wound up working in a musty bookstore instead. He asked if she'd visited Matamoros often. She said, "Once was enough. I don't speak Spanish and some fresh cowboy pinched my bottom!"

He managed not to laugh. Her words did not discourage him all that much. The goat-grinned kids who pinched bottoms on the street didn't seem capable of grasping how stupid they were acting. He had it on good authority that whores on the prowl rejected bottom-pinching assholes as undesirable trade. Choosing his own next moves with way more care, Longarm casually pointed out that it looked like rain and asked whether she wanted to head back to her boardinghouse or mayhaps somewhere more . . . private.

She pretended not to follow his meaning, bless her schoolmarm soul, and allowed it might be best to get back to Madame Belle's if it was fixing to rain. So he settled their tab, leaving a dime tip at both their places, and gallantly offered her his left elbow as they stepped out into the gathering dusk. Longarm caught a flash of something dimly lit but likely white crabbing sideways down the quay a hundred yards or so. So they'd had that same jasper tail him from the boardinghouse? What in thunder were they expecting him to do when they weren't looking—get laid?

Longarm was too good a sport to pout about it and he wanted to leave a clean taste in Velma Oakhurst's memories, so he went on behaving as if they were still sparking, even though, in point of fact, he'd given up on her as too much trouble for any possible gain.

He no longer cared whether she was inexperienced or playing hard-to-get. He knew that no matter what he got it was only going to be, at best, a good piece of ass. After that, if he was any judge of womankind, parting figured to be protracted and painful. He could already hear the mousy-haired little shop clerk pissing and moaning about the way she'd been used and abused and, after that, using and abusing her under old Belle Lasalle's roof sounded complexicated.

The picture of old Belle creeping in late at night to

126

join the two of them in his hired bedstead was only tempting until a man considered what the both of them were likely to call him.

But they'd only gone a short way when the overcast sky above opened wide to rain fire and salt on the lower valley of the Rio Grande. The two of them were half-soaked by the time Longarm dragged the surprised Velma under the shelter of a covered archway facing the suddenly deserted waterfront. As she stood there gazing out in wonder with strands of her mousy hair unpinned and plastered down the front of her wet face Velma sobbed, "Oh, Lord, how are we ever going to get home?"

He said, "It ain't that far and it's raining too hard for it to last. We're enjoying what you call a line-squall, a curtain of rain sweeping ahead of a change in the weather. I sure hope we're talking about cooler instead of hotter."

They were joined in the deep shadows under the arches by a shorter figure wearing a rain-soaked planter's hat of white straw. There was nothing in the constitution forbidding a stranger from coming in out of the rain, so Longarm said nothing, even as the pest edged past as if to stand on the far side for whatever reasons.

His reasons became more clear as he suddenly purred, *"Buenas noches, El Brazo Largo,"* followed, in Border Mex, by advice not to go for that six-gun at his side.

So as Longarm casually turned with a puzzled smile to ask, *"¿Hablas a mi, amigo?"* He shot the stranger point-blank with the double derringer he'd had palmed in his right fist since spotting that first flash of white.

It was still a near thing. The Colt .38-Short Detective Special in the Mexican's hand got off one shot by dying reflex as he went flying backward. But fortunately there was just no saying where his last wild round hit. Then Longarm was dragging the weeping and wailing Velma

127

down the archway and into a shop at the far end, closed for the night, or so it had seemed before Longarm kicked the door in, hauled Velma inside, and shoved the door shut, hoping nobody might notice a few splinters near the latch in such tricky light.

They seemed to be in a candle shop, judging from the smell of scented wax and the wares dangling betwixt them and the front window. Velma sobbed, "Oh, my Lord, I know you had to shoot that Mexican who was out to rob us, Mike. But I can't afford the scandal! There are people in my family I've been trying to avoid. But if we wind up with our names in the papers . . ."

He soothed, "I don't want to be in the papers any more than you do, Miss Velma. And look what I just found! There's a bolt to this door as locks it on the inside. So any copper badges trying doors along this arcade should be satisfied we're closed for the night."

"You mean we don't have to tell anyone?" she gasped, hopefully.

To which he replied, throwing the bolt, "Not if we don't care to. We can just sit tight in here 'til things calm down outside. We have this place to ourselves for as long as we might need it, this side of sunrise."

Chapter 15

Despite the wind and rain that single shot brought the law and a heap of others running. As Longarm had feared, somebody rattled the door of the candle shop. As Longarm had hoped, they moved on as if satisfied when the door appeared securely locked for the night. But he suggested they'd best move into the back, lest some nosey pest come by with a bull's-eye lantern to peer in through the front glass.

Nobody lived in the back, of course, but like most such shops, this one was set up with a wash basin and crapper, a charcoal brazier for light cooking and a leather chesterfield sofa big enough for a lie-down when business was slow.

Knowing better than to strike any lights, they sat side by side in their damp duds, barely able to make one another out in the light from the back windows. But she sounded as if she was crying as she went on about just hating Texas and its brutal ways. She said hardly anybody ever got robbed by Mexicans where she'd grown up.

Dying for a smoke, or *something* to do with his hands,

Longarm broke open and reloaded his derringer by feel as he casually asked her why she had to dwell in Brownsville if she hated it so much.

She said she'd already told him and made him wish he'd kept his mouth shut by launching into that all too familiar tale told by the black sheep, male and female, of many a prim and proper late Victorian family. The only difference, in her case, was that she'd gotten in trouble running up bills when her stingy stepfather had refused to increase her allowance. She said her real dad and his family had been a whole lot more easygoing whilst she'd been growing up. Then her dear old dad had died and her mom had remarried a skinflint neighbor, likely in desperation, whilst Velma had been in her early teens.

She said her stepdad had whupped her once and tried to settle her overdrawn credit around town by trying to crawl into bed with her one night when her mom had been down with the ague.

Longarm wasn't surprised to hear she'd helped herself to household funds in a cookie jar and decamped the next morning. He probed just enough to establish her as nineteen, going on twenty, and learn she'd come to Texas after knocking about other parts of the West in hopes of meeting long lost kin on her dead dad's side.

When that hadn't panned out she'd perforce taken that job selling books and found herself stuck there, in a climate she couldn't abide, surrounded by folk that scared her.

She said, "I do mean to get out of Brownsville as soon as I save up some money, Mike. I do make a tad more than my room and board at Madame Belle's costs me. But I can't leave until I have enough set aside to tide me over whilst I find a job out California way. That's where I'd like to end up. This girl I met who'd been out

130

to San Francisco told me it never gets really hot or cold out there."

He said, before he'd thought, "It's all right if you don't mind fog and all-day drizzles, come wintertime."

He silently cussed himself when she asked, "Oh, have you been out to San Francisco, too? Madame Belle was saying you came from Utah Territory. What were you doing out in California, Mike?"

He said, "A little of this and a dab of that. You might describe me as a sort of contractor, Miss Velma."

"You mean you build things?" she asked.

He said, "Sometimes there's as much money in tearing things down. I suspect that jasper out front thought I had some money on me, just now."

She repressed a shudder and replied, "He surely picked the wrong couple to rob! What was that he called you in Spanish, just before you had to shoot him?"

Longarm shrugged and said, "Something about my being taller than him, as best I can follow the lingo my ownself. If he was so worried about being a head shorter than a man with a six-gun on his hips you'd have expected him to pester somebody smaller."

"Do you think they're liable to find out about our part in all that noise going on out front?" she asked in a worried tone.

Longarm said, "Depends on who he was. If he was a known stick-up artist the law won't waste much time on his demise. If he turns out to be . . . well, a bounty hunter who made a gross mistake, there might be some copper badges canvassing the neighborhood. But nobody else could have witnessed what happened, or we'd have already heard some pounding on the door out front. So, like I said, neither one of us has to see our names in the papers unless we want 'em there."

She sighed and said, "I hope so. I'd die if my snooty

131

kith and kin back home ever read about my being involved in a waterfront shooting in Texas! Whyever might one of those gunmen interested in collecting rewards have bothered you like that, Mike?"

Longarm as Mormon Mike soberly replied, "I just now said he didn't have just cause to pester me, anywhere in Texas. So let's hope he was just what he appeared to be, a stick-up artist trying to take advantage of a couple seeking shelter in a storm."

She laughed softly and answered, "I never expected to break into a shop with you! Are you sure there aren't some things about you that a girl might need to know before she . . . got to know you better?"

He answered, truthfully enough when you read the small print, that he'd never done anything he was all that ashamed of and added that when people didn't like him the way he was they could leave him alone.

So she cuddled closer to assure him she hadn't been trying to intimate he wasn't worth knowing better.

He figured that was as good a time to kiss her as she was likely to offer. When he took her in his arms to do so she kissed back with more passion than he'd expected from a mousy-headed bookstore gal. So one friendly feeling led to another until he had her damp skirts up around her waist with her bare behind hauled foreward on the damp leather to meet him as he dropped his jeans and six-gun, kneeling betwixt spread thighs whilst she stammered, "No, wait, I mean I want to, but what if somebody comes?"

She laughed sort of dirty and spread her thighs friendlier when he told her he sure hoped both of them might manage that. But even though she screwed back with enough experience to leave Longarm's conscience clear, he was just as glad he wouldn't be stuck there in Brownsville another full day.

It wasn't that he'd carried out his mission. He barely had a handle on the Tiger Lady and her paid assassins. But a gambler who stayed in the game after six-guns had been placed on the table was a gambler who needed his head examined.

He'd been spotted by somebody local who'd turned him in for the Mex reward. He had no way of knowing who or what he might be up against in Brownsville. So it was time to get out of Brownsville. It was simple as that. He'd just tell them at the boardinghouse he'd booked safe passage to climes more healthy for the fictitious Mormon Mike and let somebody else see if they could manage the investigation once he'd withdrawn gracefully with the game still in progress.

By the time they'd gone about as far as they cared to with half their duds on, the noise and rain outside had died down a heap. When he tried to unbutton her bodice Velma murmured, "Not here, dear. It seems so sordid on this sticky leather and I'd rather get naked with you between clean sheets on a regular bed. What if we were to sort of sneak on back to the boardinghouse and . . . you know."

He pointed out, "They'd know. Ain't no way we could hope to pussyfoot in together, late as this, without anybody listening outside your door or mine. Make more sense if we were to duck out yonder back door and check into a hotel for the night."

When she asked what kind of a girl would check into a hotel with a man he said, "Neat and tidy, come morning. If we hired a honeymoon suite with a bath and hung these duds on hangers to dry, I could walk you to work in the morning after we'd both had a bath and shared my comb."

She asked what they'd think at the boardinghouse.

He said, "What they might think and what they might

know for certain are two different matters entirely. No-body there will be able to say they saw us come in to-gether at an unseemly hour."

So, as he figured she might, she agreed to do things his way, up to the time she got him in a hotel bed with some ways of her own she wanted to try.

She said she'd never done it in a tub before and al-lowed there was much to be said about finishing up down yonder with a soap-slicked dick and a good rinse-out, afterwards.

They had breakfast in bed at the hotel as part of the honeymoon deal. Then he walked her to work when the streets were more crowded and helped her open up, be-hind the book stacks, before he strolled back to the board-inghouse, arriving just before nine.

They'd finished breakfast by then. He still scouted Ma-dame Belle up to tell her he was fixing to leave town. She wisfully confessed she'd missed him the night before but neither argued nor offered to return a dime of the room and board he'd paid in advance.

It was Tom Corrigan who came up to his hired front room to say, "Belle just told me. Let me guess. That *was* you who shot it out with Jesus Garcia last night along the waterfront, right?"

"Who might Jesus Garcia be?" asked Longarm as Mor-mom Mike.

Corrigan answered easily, "Well known and justly feared bounty hunter here along the border. Brought 'em in dead or alive on both sides of the same, depending on where they were wanted. So those low bounty fliers you have in your saddle bag ain't the whole story, after all. You're wanted more serious in other places."

Longarm commenced to pack his saddle bags with the possibles he'd strewn about the room as he replied, "If you say so. Thought I might as well leave town before

134

anyone else points a fool .38-Short at a grown man."

Corrigan said, "Don't get your bowels in an uproar. You're safe enough up here and Juan Pablo Jones will be back soon with a deal as may interest you. How's you like to leave town and make some money at the same time, Mormon Mike?"

"Who do I have to kill?" replied Longarm as Mormon Mike in that same mocking tone.

The older man soberly replied, "Juan Pablo will have the details if the client's approved the changes. Juan Pablo can finger the target but they'd never stand for a Mex picking a fight with a big-shot mining man in a Colorado location run by Anglos. We'd told Solitaire Stryker to drift up yonder discreet and wait for Juan Pablo to join him. You know how discreet the hashish smoking asshole was and he gave us all a hell of a scare when they picked him up before he had the railroad soot washed out of his hair. Our client was afraid they'd send somebody down here to arrest us all. Gleason and Bunny Weed headed the famous Longarm off. But our client was still scared and suspicious of you."

"Is that how come you assigned me to Juan Pablo's job down Mexico way?" asked Longarm, casually.

Tom Corrigan made no bones about it, nodding to confess, "Juan Pablo couldn't have done a better job down yonder, you hell-for-leather cuss. Juan Pablo still had reservations about you, feeling sensitive as he does about Anglo lawmen considering anyone south of the border sort of expendable. But he had to admit no undercover lawman would have call to tangle with a licensed bounty hunter. 'Soose Garcia never would have draw on you if you hadn't been on one of his wanted lists."

Longarm shrugged and said, "If you're trying to get me to own up to that shooting it ain't going to work. How do I know *you* ain't some undercover lawman, trying to trick me into saying things I might well regret some day? Have you been shooting anyone for me to hold over you, in return?"

Tom Corrigan laughed boyishly and decided, "You are really something else, Mormon Mike! What do you take me for, some sort of pimp? It was me as shot that remount officer up to Fort Stockton last May. It would hardly be ethical for me to tell you just who paid for our services. But if you'd settle for a hint, never aid and abet the theft of army stock with a nosey superior riding herd on your books."

Longarm recalled the case. It was federal as well as yet to be solved, officially. But he pretended not to care as he grudgingly told Corrigan, "Do I miss my coastal steamer, I'll have to leave town by train and they might be watching at the station, now that some person or persons unknown has gunned that bounty hunter."

Corrigan insisted, "Juan Pablo knows more ways in and out of town than the Texas Rangers might consider possible. When you have greaser kith and kin on both sides of the border you don't need to use public roads in such flat country. Do the two of you ride some, changing mounts as you coffee and cake at *ranchos* where nobody will ever remember your passing, you can board a Denver-bound train well clear of Brownsville and be on your way in high style. The client's paying transportation expenses, seeing the target's so far from country we usually work in."

Longarm as Mormon Mike said he'd study on the offer but went on with his packing. Corrigan got him to say he'd wait as long as noon and have a last supper, at least, before he ran off with the bit in his teeth.

He agreed, but didn't have to wait that long. Juan Pablo Jones got back a little after ten to say it looked as if they'd be heading up to Denver around sundown. He

136

didn't say who was working what out with that skittish client. Longarm didn't ask. He had their table of organization figured tight enough to round up the important ones. Lesser lights, such as chambermaids who delivered envelopes or Mex fisherfolk who ran informal ferry crossings could usually be counted on to turn states evidence in exchange for a walk in the sunshine. So all he needed was solid evidence of a criminal conspiracy on his own side of the border. He knew Billy Vail would prefer a criminal conspiracy that could be tried in the Denver District Court. Longarm had no power to arrest Doñas Inez for conspiring to murder Don Hernan had there really been a murder and, what the hell, what was done was done and the world was well rid of the arrogant mean drunk and his deadly bodyguard.

But whether the mining man someone in Texas wanted murdered up in Colorado was a swell guy or as big a pain in the ass as Don Hernan, it just wouldn't do to let the Tiger Lady arrange for such a grim future for an American citizen, even if she did serve a tolerable breakfast in bed for a gent she seemed to prefer alive, so far.

Chapter 16

The sun was out some more. But it was still cool enough to read in his hired room about geology, seeing they might be sending him after a mining man, this time.

As he waited it came to him that the Tiger Lady didn't sit like a spider in her web, waiting for folk with someone in their way to find her. What had it so tough for the law to get the goods on her was that she and her pals found the clients.

Running at least this boardinghouse, a genteel tearoom and a fortune-telling operation south of the border, they lay in wait for tales of woe you'd expect to hear in such surroundings, sized up the client and his or her ability to pay, then, just as they recruited killers with the use of their one or more safe hiding places, they approached the client with the deal. In both cases taking their own sweet time lest they trust the wrong stranger.

Corrigan had intimated the job up Denver way had been an unusual contract for a bunch based astraddle the border. Longarm felt he could be fairly certain that a target that far off meant someone from up yonder had come to Brownsville, mayhaps Matamoros, on other business and been approached by the Tiger Lady. Nobody in Colorado would have heard tell there were killers for hire down this way and come calling with any hope of finding toad squat. So once he found out who the intended victim was, it might be easier to narrow the field of likely enemies to some two-face shopping for cactus candy and straw *vaqueros* down this way.

Nobody had told him anything more by noon. Velma Oakhurst came home from her bookstore for dinner and sat there as if butter wouldn't melt in her mouth through the chicken gumbo and Crappy Susan dessert whilst Longarm as Mormon Mike was perishing for lack of coffee and an after-dinner smoke.

Suspecting she'd think him rude if he avoided her, he waited on the veranda steps and it was there she joined him on her way back to work after changing to a fresh summer frock and splashing toilet water all over and doubtless up her.

As he rose to tick his hat brim to her, Velma murmured in a hurt tone, "They say you're leaving this evening. Will I have a chance to . . . see you before you have to go?"

Longarm as Mormon Mike sighed sincerely and said, "I'll likely be in the company of a traveling companion. If so, it won't be for me to set the exact time of departing and we'd best set tender feelings aside 'til we get back."

"Oh, you'll be coming back to me?" she brightened.

That seemed close enough. He told her, "I'll likely have to, if it all works out as planned. Just have to ride out of town a ways on a business errand. We can talk about it once I get back."

She glanced about as if to make certain they weren't to be overheard before she whispered, "What's this all about, Mike? Are you up to something shady? You can trust me!"

139

He smiled down fondly and allowed, "I know. I was there last night when you had the chance to turn me in. But ask me no questions, I'll tell you no lies, and we can talk about what I might or might not do for a living when I get back."

"I have a right to know what sort of man I might be getting serious with!" she protested.

He agreed she sure did and left it for her to figure how serious they were getting. So she flounced off to work, cussing under her breath about all men.

It was getting stuffy upstairs, so he sat alone on the steps. Less than an hour later, Juan Pablo Jones rode in from town on a bay barb, leading a bareback buckskin of the same Hispano-Moorish breed.

Reining in and dismounting with his split bell-bottoms swishing, the Tex-Mex rider held on to his reins and the lead line as he told Longarm, "I figured you'd want to use that Anglo stock saddle in your room. Get it and let's ride. I'll tell you about it along the way."

Longarm as Mormon Mike didn't say Corrigan had told him they'd be leaving around sundown. The siesta hours were a good time to ride across Tex-Mex spreads, too, and shy little darlings who kept changing their plans would be bitches to set up in advance for.

Nobody inside Madame Belle's seemed to be there to bid him *adios*. So they knew he and Juan Pablo were leaving, bless their coy hides.

As Longarm saddled the buckskin with that borrowed roper loaded up with his possibles and Winchester '73 he casually asked where they might be headed.

Juan Pablo Jones said, "We'll have plenty of time to talk about it, long before we get there. So let's get going."

They did. Juan Pablo led the way north through a Tex-Mex neck of Brownsville where none of the few folk on the street during *la siesta* seemed to look their way.

They rode out of town through modest fields of tall corn and knee-high pepper or bean bushes. Spanish-speaking truck farmers grew heaps of both and neither had set fruit yet. The housing they passed, unlike that further up the Rio Grande, was wood frame or woven wattle instead of adobe, which tended to melt like ice cream in the humid air of the lower valley. They rode past many a spread devoted to pigs and chickens, which Spanish-speaking folk preferred over beef, and then as they rode out past an easy haul into the Brownsville produce market, they passed kids herding goats and long-horns grazing unattended in the low chaparral spread like a thick-pile carpet as far as the eye could see to the north.

That was six or eight miles from the advantage of a saddle, Longarm knew. *Chaparral* was a Spanish word that went with Spanish grazing habits. It literally meant scrub oak but applied to all the kinds of sticker-brush that could bear up to heavier grazing than you saw in an average English meadow painted by Mister John Constable. Some said the wild romantic heather of the Scotch Highlands had resulted from the same overgrazing of range held in common by rival stockmen. The chaparral this close to the gulf ran to sandburrs, seagrape, Spanish bayonet and such instead of greasewood, sagebrush and such, with more grass growing thicker betwixt the thorny clumps.

After a spell a rooftop rose over the northern horizon and two hours later they were on their way again on fresh mounts after a tortilla snack, with Juan Pablo hogging all the coffee, damn it.

Longarm as Mormon Mike couldn't tell whether the young Tex-Mex gunslick was just closemouthed by nature or suspicious as he waited, and waited some more, to hear tell about their mission.

They rode all day and into the night, changing mounts half a dozen times and enjoying a set-down supper at a big cattle spread where nobody seemed to care what their names might be.

Then, along about midnight in the railroad town of Cameron, Texas, they left the ponies they'd been riding with yet more Tex-Mex associates and boarded a north-bound night train, with Juan Pablo springing for a private compartment.

As they stowed their baggage behind the locked corridor door, Juan Pablo said, "We don't leave this hidey-hole for food, drink or pussy. We can send out for food and drink. You'll have to care for your other needs. I've spent some time in prison but I never adjusted that way to my cell mates."

"That makes two of us," chuckled Longarm, as an owl-hoot rider with a record, adding, "I always figured that once they turned you into a jailhouse queer they'd won, by breaking your old habits to new ones."

They sat down across from one another, with no lamp alight, so's they could admire the moonlight on the range outside as their night train picked up speed. Longarm didn't give a shit about Juan Pablo's private habits, but the lithe young killer droned on about liking to get such things straight, early on. He said, "Had to kill another kid I was hiding out with one time when he just couldn't keep his hands on his own *piton*. So I ask you, do I look like a *maricon* to you?"

"You're just naturally pretty," Longarm soothed, suggesting, "Let's agree we each get to jack ourselves off and change the subject. When do I see my front money for this job in Denver?"

The Tex-Mex replied without thinking, "The job's in the mining town of Golden, just west of the state capital. There's this safe-deposit box in this bank in Denver. I

142

have a key. But there's nothing in it right now. Somebody else on their way to Denver by other means will leave envelopes for both of us there, once the *Rocky Mountain News* carries the story of a fatal shoot-out up in Golden."

"You mean I don't see nothing in advance, this time?" Longarm griped as Mormon Mike.

Juan Pablo explained, "They thought you'd need convincing on your first job for us and, to tell the truth, that was a test. Had you been less than advertised, or some two-faced sneak, you'd have taken the money and run, or tried to. We were watching pretty tight."

Longarm as Mormon Mike snapped, "Never mind ancient times. I don't like this at all! Reminds me of them advertised sales where you get there to take advantage of that real bargain and they tell you they've sold all them Stetson hats for a dollar but stand ready to sell you something better for two! How do I know I'll be paid at all for this job in Golden? Who do they want me to pick a fight with and how much am I going to get for winning one?"

Juan Pablo soothed, *"Espérate. Todavia esta temprano.* We have plenty of time and might be best if you know less until is time for to make you move, eh?"

Longarm, as the hot-tempered gunslick he'd invented, spat, *"Estás lleno de mierda, pendejo!* And your switching accents, hoping to get out of answering simple questions don't cut no ice with this child. I ain't about to play kid games with a grown-up hangman hovering in the foggy, foggy dew you're blowing in my face. If you don't trust me, *chingae tu madre* and I'm getting off at the next stop, hear?"

Juan Pablo murmured in a dangerously sleepy tone, to those who knew border ways, "Watch that shit about my mother and don't pick up your marbles just yet. They

143

don't want *me* in any shape to tell the law too much if things go wrong. Haven't you tumbled to the way we get further instructions along the way, yet? I know we're to share fifteen hundred, even, if it's all the same with you, once it appears in the papers that a hot-tempered Colorado big shot who's already killed his man in an affair of honor, lost another such dust-up in his sporting house out Golden way. I'm not even sure for certain which of two partners our client wants you to shoot it out with. There'll be a letter waiting once we get there, in care of Denver General Delivery."

Longarm as Mormon Mike stared thoughtfully out at the dull scenery under the Texas stars as he mused, as if half to himself, "I was up that way one time. The mines in Golden have bottomed out. There's the Colorado School of Mines operating over on the slopes of Lookout Mountain, these days. Ain't no going gold mines left. So somebody is full of shit about our target."

Juan Pablo sounded relieved as he explained, "Ah that's easy, look you! Tom Corrigan told me how these two partners made out mining copper in Tennessee before they came West to prospect in the Rockies and discovered how much more there was to be made selling supplies and a chance to double one's winnings in the more comfortable surroundings of their Golden Chance Casino, you see."

Longarm grunted as if still pissed, hiding how pleased he was, now that he'd narrowed it down so tight. He had the name of a saloon run by two partners from back East. It was still too early to arrest Juan Pablo Jones, but as the kid had just said, they had plenty of time to work with. It might even be possible to slicker the gang further if he could get Juan Pablo to wait in Denver for him whilst he rode on out to Golden with the name of the partner he was supposed to kill.

From their choosing first Solitaire Stryker and then his fictitious gunfighter, Mormon Mike, it sounded as if the intended target, like the late Don Hernan Vasquez Padilla, had a rep for noisy showdowns. But a born duelist in a rough trade would hardly be likely to have a milktoast as a business partner. So farther along, as the song had it, he might know more about it.

And so things went for the next few tedious days of railroad travel in the company of a man who killed for profit or whenever anybody pissed him off, it appeared.

But Longarm was just as content to stay cooped up in compartments as they transfered from line to line, working ever closer to parts where he was known better as Longarm than as Mormon Mike. He suggested and was pleased to have the Tex-Mex agree it might be best if he holed up when they got to Denver and Juan Pablo went to the general post office for further directions. Longarm was well-known around Golden as well, having shot it out on that butte just east of town a spell back. But if he could get Juan Pablo to hole up and wait for him in Denver, things might still work out.

But they never made it to Denver together. They'd just boarded yet another pullman combination in the southeast Colorado stop at Springfield Junction when things went to hell in a hack.

The conductor who came to their compartment to punch their tickets meant well and was only trying to be friendly when he smiled down at a lawman he knew to say, "Afternoon, Longarm, what brings you down this way this morning?"

Knowing Juan Pablo Jones was sure going to want to know the same answers, Longarm was already going for his cross-draw .44-40 as the Tex-Mex rose, slapping down at his buscadero side-draw without a word of further discussion.

It was too close for comfort, but Longarm packed his six-gun cross-draw because he could get at it just as well sitting down. So he fired up into the man with the faster holster, from a standing position, in the time it took even a desperate man to stand up.

Juan Pablo collapsed like a punctured hot water bottle to sprawl back in his own seat, pissing the green plush as he stared up at the compartment lamp with a dreamy smile.

The bewildered conductor, cowering against the door-jamb with his ticket puncher raised as a piss-poor shield, stammered, "What happened? Did I say something wrong?"

To which Longarm could only reply in a weary tone, "If you hadn't, somebody else would have, sooner or later. So now this one old boy has lost and I'll be whupped with snakes if I don't fear the Tiger Lady's won this round from me!"

Chapter 17

Crossing state lines in uncertain times, the railroads of the day hired their own private police forces, the Pinkertons in the case of that particular line. So Longarm got the conductor to fetch 'em and, though he didn't cotton to telling them as much as he had to, he had to if he expected them to go along with some unusual law enforcement.

He had to remind one he was a federal official and ask everybody to consider how much federal open range their tracks lay across. But in the end they saw fit to smuggle the body forward at the next water stop, keep it on ice near the dining car, and let him worry about having it removed by other federal deputies a flag-stop shy of Denver.

He sent the wire from a dispatch shed at the water stop whilst the train crew moved the tarp-wrapped cadaver of Juan Pablo up alongside the cars on the siding as the foreward tender took on tower-water.

He got off at Castle Rock along with what was left of Juan Pablo Jones. Billy Vail in the flesh had come down with a canvas-topped ambulance drawn by six good mules and as soon as the deputies with him had spirited the dead assassin off the train and out of sight the older lawman took Longarm aside to say, "Let them smuggle your impounded evidence to an unmarked drawer in the Denver Morgue, the hard way. We can catch the next northbound local and beat them into town by hours."

So, rank having its privileges, the two senior lawmen repaired to a trackside saloon to catch up on the case over suds and salted nuts after sending the dead Tex-Mex on his way.

It didn't take long to have Billy Vail cussing morose. Once they'd made it to his having to shoot it out with Juan Pablo Jones aboard that last train, Vail cussed like a mule skinner with a toothache and said, "So we get to cut and shuffle a whole new hand because that Tiger Lady has played that last hand too slick for us, if she's really the one in charge, down yonder."

Longarm washed down some nuts and said, "I'm pretty certain she's calling the shots and I ain't so sure she's all that smart. *Cautious* is the word I'd use. I'll be surprised if she doesn't turn out to have a prison record, as an Anglo, Cajun or Creole gal from somewhere close to New Orleans, where she met Madame Belle and that shy little sneak, Monique. One way or another, our mysterious Tiger Lady wound up with a town house, a boardinghouse and a fashionable teahouse north of the border crossing. Taking an interest in hocus pocus, she'd have been reading tea leaves as Cora Martin some of the time and dealing Tarot cards in Matamoros as La Dama Tigra aka Señora Martinez at others. It's too early to say whether they planned it from the beginning or just saw an opportunity and grabbed for it. Either way, a boardinghouse in a border town attracted Tom Corrigan and other knockaround drifters about the time the Tiger Lady noticed how many of her clients had both money to spend and bigger problems than one can solve with tea leaves or Tarot cards."

"Are you saying most of their customers have been women pissed off at their husbands?"

Longarm shrugged and said, "Tom Corrigan is a natural conversationalist with plenty of time on his hands. There's no telling who or how often he'd encounter a prospective male customer. We know he's been recruiting sinister young gents with no visible means of support to make tea-leaf and Tarot card predictions come true. Like I said, the operation hasn't been all that fiendishly *clever*. Just careful. Nobody's been *advertising* an assassination service on either side of the border. For every contract they've agreed to they've surely heard dozens of sob stories from lesser lights with neither the gumption nor the money to be offered a simple solution. Having met up with the wife of the late Don Hernan, I can easily see how she might have pissed and moaned all over Matamoros about the mean bastard before she found out you could cross a gypsy's hand with a little extra silver and get shed of the him without having to go back to being poor."

"You reckon somebody like that sent you and the late Juan Pablo up this way to murder . . . whomsoever?"

Longarm sipped more suds, considered ordering a cigar from the bar, and decided to stay Mormom Mike a spell as he told his secret boss, "I don't see how it could be a wife or mistress. From the little I've been able to put together, the client, this time, seems to be lurking nearby, anxious to see somebody in Colorado dead, but nervous as all hell about the deal. The job was supposed to have been done by Solitaire Stryker, as you may recall."

Vail grimaced and said, "He's got his own nerves back under control. He hung his fool self in his cell when we

149

wouldn't let him have any more hashish. You never read it in the papers because it ain't been in the papers. It's easy to keep things quiet when your swell pals never send one lawyer or bail bondsman to comfort you!"

Longarm soberly pointed out, "They were banking on my getting shot in Parsons Junction breaking the daisy chain back to them. They must have figured he was fixing to hang no matter what they tried to do for him, so they let him hang. That's likely why they bought the notion of that other gunslick they sent to the junction after me just lighting out for parts unknown. I wonder if Juan Pablo was really fixing to pay me off in cash or some other way, once I gunned that target in Golden for their customer in Texas."

"We'll never know unless we figure out who you were supposed to gun in Golden," Vail pointed out, adding, "There's no way we can open up to the both of them. Not before we find out what one partner might have to gain from the sudden demise of the other!"

Longarm sighed and said, "I know you think you taught me everything I know, Boss. But that was unkind. I'd already figured on picking up a letter addressed to Juan Pablo in care of General Delivery at the Denver General Post Office. With any luck it ought to tell us who they want Mormon Mike to pick a fight with, out Golden way."

So they finished a few more beers and boarded a north-bound local for Denver within the hour. Seeing he'd been buried out by Camp Weld, officially, Billy Vail had Longarm wait in the back room of the Black Cat near the station while he mosied over to the post office.

Having already introduced Mormon Mike to cold lager and seeing he was more likely to meet folk who knew him as Longarm from here on in, the lawman left to twiddle his thumbs in the Black Cat ordered coffee instead of more beer and enjoyed the first three-for-a-nickel cheroot he'd dared to light in days.

He'd expected it to taste better. Kissing a gal who'd put you through a couple of hoops too many could be a letdown, too.

He'd just taken to wondering what could be keeping Billy Vail when his boss grumped back in, muttering dreadful things about the postmaster general.

When Longarm asked how come, Vail said, "They didn't have no letters addressed to a Juan Pablo Jones. That Tiger Lady of yours has wrapped one damned layer of deception after another around her devious core. Peel one layer away and there you are with another one to peel off!"

Longarm suggested, "Wouldn't take a college degree in deception to see the advantages of Juan Pablo picking up his general delivery mail as a Smith instead of Jones."

Billy Vail snorted, "Now who's being unkind about another lawman's common sense? I naturally asked them to show me all the mail they had postmarked from Brownsville or mayhaps Matamoros. They told me they got lots of mail from Texas, close as they are to the Denver Stockyards, and suggested I seek a court order if I aimed to paw through heaps of mail addressed to anyone I couldn't name."

Longarm suggested, "The post office would be closed long before we could ever get a court order, if we could get a court order at this hour. I still have the safe-deposit key Juan Pablo was packing, but the banks are already closed if I was certain which bank we were talking about."

Billy Vail wound up to say something mean about banks.

But Longarm said, "Don't get your bowels in an uproar. The day may be dying but the cool shades of eve-

151

ning have yet to get started and I could get out to Golden by narrow guage in little more than an hour."

"As whom?" asked the older lawman, "Your true self or as the famous Mormon Mike?"

Longarm decided, "Whichever works best, depending on who I meet up with. I've never been Mormon Mike this far north of the border and I know some folk in Golden to howdy. But it might be best to play it with my cards close to my chest for, like you said, it seems one damned onion skin of deception under another, with the little I've been told shifting every time you peel away another!"

He blew a thoughtful smoke ring, stared soberly through it at his boss, and said, "They tell it one way. Then they tell it another way. The client wants me to gun a mining man up Denver way, then he turns out to be a saloon keeper twenty miles off to the west. For all I know for certain they could have sent me after a whorehouse piano player at the behest of that shoeshine boy I told you about."

Vail smiled dubiously and said, "He'd have to shine a whole lot of shoes or have a great line of credit. What was that you said about a safe deposit key, again?"

Longarm said, "I told you. My Tex-Mex mentor said that once they read in the papers about my gunfight out to Golden they'd have somebody leave fifteen hundred dollars in that safe-deposit box for Juan Pablo to pick up. Knowing what a tough time Juan Pablo would have with that chore I relieved him of the key. I'm still working on which bank they had in mind."

Vail said, "Give it to me. I can find out by way of the banking commission from its serial number."

Longarm fished the safe deposit key from his change pocket but warned as he handed it over, "It might be best to stake the bank out discreet, once you locate it. You don't know any of the gang on sight. How can you hope to arrest anybody sneaking money *in* to a bank?"

Vail said, "We don't have to, until later, after we've esablished someone tried to pay that well for a killing. I had a box camera in mind, set up across the way, with someone in the bank signaling each and every time an unfamiliar face who wasn't a regular customer left from the vicinity of their safe-deposit boxes. Before you ask how we can afford that many photo plates, consider how many total strangers hire safe-deposit boxes in your average bank."

Longarm nodded thoughtfully and decided, "That only works after a total stranger, or an associate of the Tiger Lady who dwells here moves to pay Mormon Mike off for killing . . . Somebody. How do you figure I'll ever manage that, even if I figure out who they want Mormon Mike to kill, without my killing anybody?"

Vail said, "Same way we managed to let them kill you, down to Parsons Junction, of course. What good are deputy coroners and newspaper reporters if they won't do favors for their pals? Get your ass out to Golden, figure out which partner at the Golden Chance your pals in Texas want you to have a word with, and then have a word with him, in private. Do I really have to tell a sneak like you how to hide out a few days whilst we issue reports about his death and the ongoing investigation?"

Longarm said, "You do. I just said I don't know who they'd ordered me to kill and I have orders to pick a public fight with him and beat him to the draw. Would you have Mormon Mike back-shoot some poor soul in a damned dark alley?"

Vail asked, "Why not? He shot that bounty hunter in the dark without any witnesses, as far as your Tiger Lady knows. Faking a fight is a good way to beat the hangman if a killer's caught. I doubt they give a rat turd how you get away with it, as long as they can satisfy the client the victim's dead."

Longarm muttered, "You sure are asking me to debunk a legend. But I got me a narrow guage to catch. I'll wire from Golden the minute I know who Mormon Mike just shot in the back, the no-good yaller hound!" They shook on that and parted friendly.

Longarm got into Golden a little after moonrise. The erstwhile mining town of Golden nestled amid the foothills of the Front Range you could admire from Downtown Denver, a little over fifteen miles to the east. Tourists who thought you could stroll over to those pretty hills just outside of Denver tended to think Golden was named for the color once panned from the grit of Clear Creek Canyon. But in point of fact the seat of Jefferson County was named for Thomas I. Golden, a gentleman of the Hebrew persuasion, who'd laid out the first campsite along the creek back in the Colorado gold rush days.

The Golden Chance Casino stood near the busy intersection of 12th and Washington betwixt Clear Creek and the campus of the Colorado School of Mines, established a year after Longarm's Winchester '73 came out, when they were still producing plenty of gold in Golden.

The town had found new life as a county seat, a college town and, thanks to the swell water coming down Clear Creek, that swamping new brewery built by Mister Adolph Coors from Wuppertal.

Longarm had traveled light from the nearby State Capitol. So he had to pay in advance when he checked into the nearby Astor Hotel. Having set up a base of operations for the night he strode past the lit-up false front of the Golden Chance to drift on to the smaller Buffalo Rose, where a barmaid he knew was still serving suds.

They called her Ginger and she tried to live up to the

154

honor with the aid of henna rinse. When she saw Longarm bellying up to her end of the bar Ginger crossed
herself and gasped, "Jesus, Mary and Joseph and wasn't
it yourself they just murdered down in Texas the other
day and all?"

Longarm soothed, "They had me mixed up with someone as good-looking. But I'd be obliged if you didn't
spread it around. What can you tell me about those former mining men who run that Golden Chance Casino,
just the other side of Washington Avenue?"

She made a wry face and replied without hesitation,
"Not one kind word and bad cess to the both of them.
Which one might you be here to arrest, this evening,
Glass or Breedlove?"

Longarm said, "Ain't sure. Tell me more about them,
Miss Ginger."

She shrugged and replied, "What can I be after saying,
once I've said they're both dedicated bastards, cut from
the same cloth? Both have nasty tempers. It's up for
grabs whether Davie Glass or Wes Breedlove would be
faster on the draw or quicker on the trigger. I know they
say you're not bad yourself, Handsome. But if it's either
of them two you mean to go up against in their own
casino, be sure you bring along plenty of help!"

155

Chapter 18

The Golden Chance Casino was big enough inside for a barn dance, once you moved out the gaming tables and the long bar along one wall. Being situated on a corner like the Oriental in Tombstone, it came with entrances front and side, both casually guarded by gents lounging nearby in frock coats cut loose to conceal weapons.

Turning back into Mormon Mike and knowing such places discouraged the patronage of pikers with no money to spend, Longarm bought himself some blue chips to occupy his empty hands away from the bar, casually asking the flashy blonde cashier to point out Glass and Breedlove.

She said Davie Glass might be in later and pointed out Wes Breedlove in a far corner, talking to others on the far side of a roulette layout.

As Longarm drifted that way, sizing that partner up, he saw Breedlove was about the height, build and age that Honest Abe had been when *he* was assassinated. Albeit Breedlove had a mustache instead of chin whiskers. As he siddled in to join the group he heard the former mining man jawing about green donkeys and knew Breedlove hadn't entirely lost interest in mining. Mining copper, like they said he'd been at, farther east. He was explaining how the famous green donkeys of the Montana copper mines were never brought to the surface, kept slurping up mine drainage as they hauled ore trams along the tracks, and either died from the sweet copper arsinate in the water or grew green fur through their copper-impregnated hides.

Breedlove's accent was either Eastern Shore Maryland or Canadian. Two sets of Lowland Scotch had settled both widely separated parts to result in great-great-grandkids who talked like most everybody else until they got to words with OU in 'em, resulting in such oddities as "Get oot of this hoose!"

After that, despite his mean rep, Wes Breedlove seemed polite and friendly enough to the other well-dressed gents he was jawing with. Breedlove's personal frock coat hung open over a maroon brocade vest and shoulder-holstered Colt Lightning, the small-bore double-action favored by the surely overrated Billy the Kid.

As in the case of the Kid, the late Clay Allison, the Thompson boys and other reputed homicidal maniacs, Wes Breedlove in the flesh failed to look and act the part as a stage villain might have. In real life few could go about raving like lunatics very long before they got picked up and hauled off to the funny farm. Before he'd run over his fool self with a buckboard, Clay Allison had probably been the all-time nasty drunk, shooting colored cavalry troopers for no better reason than his contention that the Good Lord had never created horses to carry such sub-humans about. He'd been just as mean to many a white victim and it had been established that unlike the Kid and some others, he'd been willing to face his man and slap leather at the other's pleasure. On at least one occasion, facing up to an officer backed by a squad and daring the shavetail to fill his fist or run home to his mamma.

The officer had backed down. Yet Clay Allison had managed to operate a Colorado cattle operation sensibly enough to show a profit and hadn't beat his wife worth mention. So he must have had moments of civility and apparent common sense.

Neither of the Thompson brothers had ever gunned anybody to make money, as far as the law knew, when they weren't picking fights with good old boys who mocked their British accents. Most of the time Ben and Billy Thompson, Ben being the more dangerous, worked at honest jobs, from cattle droving to . . . come to study on it, gambling operations such as this one.

So Longarm as Mormon Mike kept his mouth shut with his ears and eyes open whilst he waited to determine which of the partners there was most likely to fit the picture painted by the late Juan Pablo Jones.

For if only one of them was the chosen target of an unknown client in Texas, the partner Mormon Mike wasn't supposed to pick a fight with could be in cahoots with the same or even running the show. It would be just as easy for a Colorado gambling man to send someone to Texas as it had been for the Tiger Lady to send not one but three private guns up to Colorado, so far.

Longarm placed a chip on the roulette layout lest somebody wonder why he was standing there like a big-ass bird. As the wheel commenced to spin at the head of the table, Longarm bet on the Double Zero, with the house.

Betting, or throwing your money away at roulette, you could bet on the bitty ball landing on a red or green, odd or even number, most of the time. If you'd picked the right slot in the wheel, the house paid off even money on red or green, odd or even, with sucker bets on pure numbers paying you thirty-five to one. So the slickery, right there in the open for the suckers to see, consisted of two extra slots, colored green instead of red or black and 0 or 00 instead of odd or even.

On an honest wheel neither came up more often than any other bets. But when they did the croupier raked in all the bets for the house, as it's open and aboveboard reasons for banking the fool game in the first place. Everybody lost, save for the house and anybody betting with the house on 0 or 00, with no side bets on red or green, odd or even.

So Longarm was surprised when he won and, not wanting to attract too much attention, he didn't rake in his big pile of chips; 0 or 00 paying thirty-five chips to his one, the same as if he'd bet one to thirty-six.

He let the bet ride, like a chump, consoling himself with the simple arithmetic that in the end he'd have only lost that one chip.

He won again. Lady Luck could be like any other woman when you only wanted her to leave you alone. As the bemused croupier took to counting out chips by stacks of ten Wes Breedlove excused himself from the bunch he'd been jawing with and stepped over to quietly suggest, "If I were you I'd quit while I was ahead, Cowboy."

Longarm could have made a swell fight of it, as Mormon Mike, but he just nodded and took off his hat, replying, "Reminds me of this time in Salt Lake City. Had this one gal waiting in my hotel room, went down to buy us a bottle, and damned if the prettiest little thing you ever did see wasn't asking my opinion on red or white wine."

As he filled the crown of his hat with chips Wes Breedlove told him he'd escort such a lucky cuss to the cashier to convert his winnings.

As they made their way through a now buzzing crowd, Longarm asked if he was being thrown out. Wes Breedlove replied in an amiable tone, "Not at all. You're still welcome at any other table in the hoose. But you've broken the bank at that one we just left. We make it a rule to extend no markers or put more hoose money into a bank that's been broken, before we total the twenty-four hoor take."

"Spoken like a true Scot," said Longarm, knowing there was no way you could insult a Scotchman by recognizing him as one.

Breedlove chuckled and said, "Close enough. My people came from a wee bit further south, ye ken, but I grew up in Nova Scotia and my late wife was Clan Donald. Would you like your winnings converted to gold or paper, Mister . . . ?"

"Mason will do for now. Mike Mason," lied Longarm, playing it safe. If Breedlove was in on the plot he'd be expecting Mormom Mike and might well open up to him. If he wasn't in on the plot no harm had been done because nobody in Colorado was hunting a desperado who didn't exist.

Breedlove told the flashy blonde to convert the more than eleven hundred dollars in chips to cash and, as she did so, offered to buy the big winner a drink at the bar.

Longarm politely declined, explaining he was a Latter-day Saint. The tall Canadian laughed boyishly, for a reputed hot temper who'd just lost that much money, and said, "I've considered converting since I heard you gents are allowed other vices. How many wives do you have to support with your reckless gambling, Mike?"

Longarm modestly replied he only had a hundred as he put away the horse-choking wad of bills the blonde

160

had secured with a rubber band. You had to wonder whether a man who'd been told they were sending a hot-tempered killer who specialized in saloon fights would insult a man's religion in a saloon, even in jest.

Seeing he wasn't likely to find out much more without asking too many obvious questions, Longarm allowed he'd be back later, once he'd put such a wad in a hotel safe for the night.

Wes Breedlove told him that sounded sensible and never asked which hotel he might be spending the night in.

There were plenty of streetlamps as well as that full moon above in a cloudless Colorado sky. So the rat-faced individual who'd followed him from the Golden Chance waited until Longarm entered the lobby of the Astor Hotel before he made his move.

Longarm had just stopped at the desk with his winnings from his sucker bet when the unshaven cuss with a big Walker Conversion gripped in both hands popped out of the shadows to whimper, "Your money or your life and I'd rather take your life!"

So Longarm threw the heavy wad of paper at his head, grabbed the long pistol barrel extended at him, and kicked the desperate but way-too-close *bandito* in the balls.

Longarm kicked him again for luck as he writhed on the lobby tiles, moaning and groaning as he clutched at his own groin. But when the night clerk gasped, "Don't let him up! I'll send the bellhop for the law!" Longarm calmly replied, "Don't ding your bell. Don't get your shit hot over nothing."

He kicked the man at his feet again to ask, "Are you going to try something else, Mister Nothing?"

The quivering wreck just cried some more as Longarm

161

bent to scoop up both the money and that ancient weapon.

Not wanting to cripple his victim total, Longarm handed the wad and the Walker across the counter, saying he'd be obliged if the clerk would keep both in the hotel safe, for now.

The clerk said he'd be proud to and asked, "What about . . . him?"

Longarm reached down to haul the subdued stick-up man to his own unsteady feet, shaking him like a naughty boy as he growled for the benefit of all present, "I'm sure he's seen the error of his ways and I have better places to be than some stuffy magistrate's court. So I reckon he's about to leave town, now, knowing that if I ever see his fucking shadow one more time, I'll kill them both."

Then he shoved his cowed victim toward the front entrance. The rat-faced individual bounced off a doorjamb, spun around, and dashed off into the night as Longarm muttered, "Pissant."

So a few minutes later, with his winnings and possible future evidence securely locked away, Longarm had a piss out back and left the Astor to head back toward the brighter lights around 12th and Washington.

As he left, the bellhop came out from the broom closet he'd ducked into to marvel, "Jesus H. Christ! What was that all about and who *is* that tall drink of water in 202?"

The clerk soberly replied, "He's registered as M. Mason from Utah Territory. He looks like a U.S. deputy marshal I've heard more about. Whoever he may be, I'd say it was best not to cross him!"

So by midnight word had gotten around the small town of Golden that a mysterious stranger called Mike Mason had broken the bank at the Golden Chance Casino, kicked the shit out of some stick-up man who'd tried to rob him, and for some reason hadn't bothered to inform

162

the law. Longarm had noticed how much they talked about you when you acted as if you didn't want them to. Out Frisco way, that crazy Englishman calling himself the Emperor Norton wandered about in an admiral's uniform and dress sword, knighting firemen and making proclamations from soap boxes as everybody pretended not to notice the poor lunatic.

He knew Ginger at the Buffalo Rose would be even more likely to tell everyone he was really Longarm if he asked her not to. So he stayed away, dining alone in a chili parlor near the tracks out from Denver as he reflected on that Texas gang's conviction that the one and original Longarm had been gunned on orders from the Tiger Lady, herself.

Conflicting rumors were an expected part of the game. He felt less conflicted about which one of the partners at the Golden Chance he was supposed to kill, now. But he wouldn't be certain until he found out whether the Davie Glass he hadn't met was American or . . . Shit, come to study on it, what if that client down along the border wanted him to gun some furriner? Where did it say no Canadian enemies or, hell, enemies left over the lost lands of Atlantis couldn't be gunning for a current resident of Colorado whilst currently residing in the lower valley of the Rio Grande?

He got back to the Golden Chance Casino just after midnight to find, as he'd hoped, Wes Breedlove had turned the operation over to the way shorter but just as smiley-faced Davie Glass.

Not wanting to seem curious, Longarm drifted over to a faro layout as if for a change of pace. The oily-haired fat boy dealing from the shoe shot an inquiring glance across the crowded room to a distant boss who didn't seem to miss much that was going on.

Davie Glass came over to politely tell Longarm their limit at that table was five thousand.

Longarm laughed lightly and replied, "I put all them early winnings, save for fifty, in my hotel safe, Mister . . . ?"

"Glass. Call me Davie Glass," replied yet another smiling cuss who was supposed to have a vicious temper. Longarm went on being Mormon Mike as he reflected on how vicious *he* was said to be. Atilla the Hun had doubtless been good to his mother. Tales of bad temper tended to grow as they were passed along, the way the dropping of a jar of olives on one corner, messy enough in its own right, could turn into a wagon load of watermelons hit by a train, a corner or so over.

Glass stayed put, even though he'd been told the lucky cuss that had broken their roulette bank wasn't betting heavy enough to win more than five thousand at faro, with the house dealing.

So they naturally swapped pleasantries, with Longarm knowing for certain he was lying about growing up out to the Mormon Delta.

He was only half listening as Davie Glass droned on about starting out around Duckville in the Tennessee copper country. Not knowing who the Tiger Lady was out to have him kill, it hardly seemed to matter that Glass, unlike his partner, the Canadian Breedlove, appeared to be American-born.

Longarm as Mormon Mike asked no questions until Glass bragged on studying mining, scientific, in college.

Longarm casually asked, "Do tell? What college might you have gone to, the mining school right here in Golden?"

Glass laughed and confessed, "I've learned more about less risky ways of making money out this way, as you can plainly see. I'm not sure the Colorado School of

Mines had been founded when I went to Penn State, back before the war."

Longarm asked, "How come? Might you be from Pennsylvania, Davie?"

Glass nodded and said. "Lancaster County, but we weren't Amish, if that's what you're so curious about."

To which Longarm soberly replied, "I ain't curious no more. I just now figured it all out. Is there somewhere we can have a word in private, Mister Glass? For you are in deep shit and we need to talk about it!"

Chapter 19

They slipped out of Golden in the wee small hours, driving back to Denver in the intended target's Studebaker buggy instead of by rail. Longarm had started to object when Glass had first suggested his own buggy. Then he'd thought better of the notion and they got to Marshal Vail's private home on Capitol Hill just as Billy was fixing to head for the office the next morning.

The three men held a council of war in Vail's kitchen whilst the motherly Mrs. Vail rustled up more buttermilk flapjacks and Arbuckle Joe. Vail said they'd be proud to put Glass up in their guest room whilst his body lay dead on ice, officially, at the morgue. Glass asked why he couldn't have a closed coffin funeral to see who might or might not think enough of him to send flowers.

Longarm said, "I'm sure the one the Tiger Lady hoped I'd kill you for would show nothing but the greatest respect and it wouldn't be fair to the ones who just like you. We can save everyone needless expense by not releasing your cadaver before we've finished our investigation."

Billy Vail said he'd cope with his fellow lodge mem-

166

ber, the Denver police commissioner. So Longarm left that and the latest victim of Mormon Mike to his boss and got cracking at his own chores.

Less than an hour later he was meeting in a side room of the Parthenon Saloon near the federal building with rival newspapermen from the *Post* and *Rocky Mountain News*. He only needed the two bigger and bitterly opposed local papers to sell his story.

Pouring a round from the scuttle of needled beer he'd ordered from the bar outside, Longarm declared, "You gents have printed wagonloads of bullshit about me in the past and you know full well I've never really sued anybody. So now I want you to print more bullshit in the interests of justice."

The portly fancy-dressing Crawford from the *Post* asked if they were talking about someone answering to his description kicking the liver and lights out of a famous stick-up man, out Golden way.

Longarm said, "We might be able to use some of that, rephrased just a tad. I'm going to lay my cards on the table faceup, provided I have your word you won't give the show away on me lest you fuck things up for your ownselves. I'm offering an exclusive on a mighty big case in the near future, in exchange for a little bullshit, here and now."

The rival reporters exchanged wary looks. When Crawford of the *Post* nodded, the smaller and more dapper Schiller of the *News* said, "This had better be good."

So Longarm told them what he wanted them to print and why, assuring them local, state and federal lawmen would be in on it, helping them make the story stick. So the rival reporters shook on the deal and lit out to have their own lies composed and run in extra editions.

That's how both the *Denver Post* and *Rocky Mountain News* came to carry the murder most foul of the late

David Glass of Golden, an old-timer generous to a fault, for all his occasional outbursts of self-defense.

His body had been found near the South Platte bridge, near his abandoned buggy and spent carriage horse. He'd been shot in the back, more than once, through his oil-cloth buggy hood, from saddle level, it would seem, leading the lawmen working on the case to suspect he'd been chased from somewhere west of town by an armed and dangerous rider.

Further investigation had just revealed that the dead proprieter of a gambling casino had had words the night before with the well-known Mormon Mike Mason, a vaguely sinister young man with no certain past nor any stated plans for the future. The *Post* and *News* almost but not quite agreed Glass might have been ill-advised to set a house limit on a man of some rep just as he seemed to be on a winning streak. But, trying to be fair, Crawford of the *Post* pointed out that Mormon Mike had been in a fight with the notorious Foxface Foley earlier that night and so it was remotely possible Mormon Mike had checked out of his hotel sudden and departed Golden without leaving any forwarding address. Reporter Crawford was reputed to be working on The Great American Novel in his spare time, too.

Meanwhile, Billy Vail's pals on the banking commission had located that safe-deposit box for them at the Drover's Trust near the Union Station. But when they went there with a search warrant, discreetly, they found the box bare as Mother Hubbard's Cupboard.

Longarm didn't need Billy Vail to point out how his Tiger Lady had likely waited until she read about it in the newspapers. Or how, once she'd dispatched some-body with the payoff, it would have to take them a spell to get there from Texas. He was more concerned with why the Tiger Lady had set things up that way to begin with.

When Vail asked him to elaborate, Longarm explained, "Mormon Mike was a loose cannon in their eyes. But Juan Pablo Jones was based along the border and would have only worked this far away from a hop, skip and a jump to Mexico for *mucho dinero*."

Vail said, "That's why they had to offer him a heap, just for pointing out Davie Glass to their triggerman, you sneaky cuss. They didn't want to pay in advance, lest they lose the money, should something go wrong. So they told that Tex-Mex to tell you—"

"I know what Juan Pablo told me," Longarm cut in, adding, "I'm still working on how come. Why didn't they just say the money would be waiting for us once we got back to Brownsville after a job well done? The Tiger Lady must have been sure she could trust Juan Pablo. He'd done tough chores for her in the past."

Vail suggested, "She might have feared you'd want to be paid off on the spot and feel free to be on your way. Would Mormon Mike have just murdered Davie Glass if he hadn't been expecting to be paid C.O.D.?"

Longarm said, "I had him register a complaint about not getting any front money on this job. But like the song says, farther along they'll send somebody with the payoff or they won't."

Vail frowned thoughtfully and asked, "Do you reckon they will? They don't know their boy, Juan Pablo, is on ice up our way, yet. How could they hope to double-cross him and stay in business?"

Longarm said, "That's what I'm worried about. They were already on the prod and shy as fat girls at a dance when I showed up after that shoot-out we misreported in Parsons Junction. I don't like to brag, but I doubt any lawman born of mortal woman could have managed to

169

get in with them the way I did if it hadn't been for heaps of shithouse luck. They tested me with that mean Mex ranchero and still wished they had Solitaire Stryker or the missing Bunny Weed to send up here with Juan Pablo. So I won't be too astonished to learn our Tiger Lady and her playmates mean to collect their last payoff and silently steal away from the mouth of the Rio Grande."

Vail asked how they were likely to find out.

Longarm said, "Stake-out. Like I said, they'll send the payoff or they won't. If they meant all along to throw Juan Pablo to the wolves we may still cut their trail out Golden way. Nobody got the Tiger Lady to have Davie Glass killed for fun. I suspect I know who and why but it can be a bitch to prove a case with no more than motive as evidence. So we'd best have a look around the Drover's Trust for a likely spot to set up our stake-out."

That turned out to be easy as pie. There was a store-front for rent catty-corner across the street from the entrance to the bank. So they made a deal with the own-ers, soaped the front window on its inside, save for a few peepholes, and made themselves comfortable, lounging in camp chairs around a folding map table with all the smokes, suds and sandwiches they needed to see them through banking hours.

Vail in the flesh could only be there part of the time, but insisted on leaving Longarm there with a four-man backup. Longarm didn't care a whole lot. A man had to take a leak now and again. But had it been up to him he wouldn't have had Deputy Thornditch posted there with him.

Edgar Thornditch was new on the job and whilst he seemed a good kid, Longarm didn't consider it a kid's chore. As he warned Thornditch and the three older dep-uties, Smiley, Dutch and Cohen, they were either likely to see no action at all, or they could find themselves up against a team of professional assassins. So he wanted one and all to pay tight attention and follow any order he might give to the fucking letter!

So, naturally, nothing happened for the first lone tedious week. Then, at nine A.M. of a Monday morning, who should come walking over from the Union Station but old Tom Corrigan, wearing a darker suit, with what seemed a doctor's leather sachel in one hand.

Longarm would have naturally let the cuss place the payoff in the safe-deposit box inside ere he made the arrest. But he made the innocent mistake of muttering, "That's him! The Tiger Lady's pal, Tom Corrigan!" and so all hell broke loose.

Longarm gasped, "No!" as young Thornditch, standing closer to the front door, flung it wide and stepped out into the street, Peacemaker drawn, cocked and leveled, to shout, "Drop that bag and grab some sky, you murdering bastard!"

The startled Corrigan whirled but held on to his prize, wailing, "I can't! Let me lower it gentle!"

So the overwrought kid deputy fired, drilling a hole through the bank window behind Corrigan, who shrilled like a housewife with a mouse up her skirt and let go his heavy bag.

It landed on the red sandstone walk by his feet, then exploded with a roar that busted both the bank windows and the plate glass Longarm was cussing behind as it blew both Corrigans legs off at the knees!

Corrigan landed on his bloody stumps to flop about like a circus seal trailing gore as it barked for fish whilst Longarm considered the way that infernal device had been designed to work.

Then he told the totally dazed Thornditch, "All right. I *ain't* going to kick the shit out of you."

"What did I just do?" gasped the kid deputy as he followed Longarm across to where Corrigan lay rapidly bleeding to death. Longarm hunkered down by the weakly blubbering Corrigan, saw he wasn't going to get any sense out of him, and told Thornditch, "You saved my life by acting like a total asshole. Had we done it my way, we'd have arrested this bozo and then I'd have gone inside, opened that safe-deposit box and look what a mess it would have made out of me!"

He asked the dying man in a conversation tone, "How was it triggered so delicate? Dynamite cap stuck in a heavy-sprung rat trap?"

Corrigan didn't answer. He was still breathing, barely, but there was nothing medical science could do for a man who'd lost so much blood.

There was no way in hell to keep *that* much excitement out of all the papers. But when Billy Vail bitched about that, later on in that side room at the Parthenon, once things had simmered down a mite, Longarm soothed, "Don't get your bowels in an uproar. What happened at the Drover's Trust this morning signed the confession with a kiss. That bomb was meant for Juan Pablo Jones. They didn't give a shit if it killed Mormon Mike or not. Once they'd read in the papers they had no further chores for their cat's paw it hardly mattered how he felt about not getting paid for his last job. The Tiger Lady figures he couldn't know where to find her. Poor Juan Pablo likely knew, but as Corrigan pointed out, an obvious Tex-Mex stands out in fancier circles north of the border and, hell, why share the pot with any more players than you have to?"

Vail asked, "Are you saying that murdersome bitch and her own inner circle will have ridden off down the Owlhoot Trail already?"

Longarm shook his head and replied, "Not hardly. La-

172

dies riding the Owlhoot Trail, sidesaddle or astride, attract attention. I can't see either Madame Belle Lasalle nor the fashionable Cora Martin tearing through the chaparral by moonlight when they have a much safer hidey-hole right there in Brownsville, or so I hope they hope!"

"You mean you know where to look for them, even with the fat in the fire, now?"

Longarm nodded soberly and said, "Unless I've been slickered way past human endurance, and a criminal genius is a contradiction in terms, I'm buying a lucky coincidence at face value. If I'm right, there's just no way the Tiger Lady could know her sucker, Mormon Mike, found out about her other address under a double identity there in Brownsville. She ought to think we have the address of that boardinghouse run by Madame Belle and one more for her fortune-telling operation across the border in Matamoros. But thanks to that one break at that bookstore I told you about, and the local city directory, I have a pretty firm handle on where the bunch of them mean to hole up, right there in town, until things cool down enough for them to simply tidy up and leave town forever, in style."

Vail said, "The rangers will want in on the last roundup. So I hope you don't make a sap out of me. What if you're wrong and your Tiger Lady has already lit out when we get there?"

Longarm shrugged and said, "In that case we can still poke around for her in the neighborhood of the one who hired her to murder old Davie Glass. His share in the Golden Chance Casino is even closer than the bunch down Texas way and sooner or later that two-face has to come foreward to harvest some ill-gotten gains."

Chapter 20

"Don't be so damned coy!" demanded Billy Vail. "If you know who paid the Tiger Lady to kill Davie Glass, spit it out!"

Longarm said, "Ain't ready to, yet. If I'm wrong I'd be making a wild false accusation. If I'm right we ought to find them all holed up in one bunch at Cora Martin's town house in Brownsville."

"Then let's haul ass for Brownsville!" whooped Billy Vail, springing to his feet.

So Longarm jumped up after them and they did. But it still seemed to take them forever to get there by rail and Longarm had to worry all the way, having less faith in himself than Vail did.

They got into Brownsville on a hot and sultry afternoon. That gave them time for some delicate negotiations and complexicated planning. The Texas Rangers wanted in. They wanted the Mex *rurales* in, despite some reservations, for the same reasons the U.S. Cav was cooperating with the Mex *federales* against Victorio and his border-jumping Apache that summer. When your barn was on fire a bucket of piss was better than nothing at all.

So the next morning, just at sunup, Texas Rangers hit Madame Belle's boardinghouse to herd everyone on the premises together in the front parlor, dressed for bed.

At about the same time other rangers and the Brownsville law busted into Cora Martin's fashionable teahouse, finding nobody there at all, whilst south of the border, now that they'd been told who'd arranged for the death of El Presidente's pal, Don Hernan Vaquez Padilla, *los rurales* proceeded to bust the shit out of *La Dama Tigra's* fortune-telling layout. They didn't get to bust the shit out of *La Dama Tigra* because they didn't find her there.

Longarm, Billy Vail and a quartet of federal deputies from Brownsville's own federal building failed to find her as Cora Martin when they busted through the front and back doors to scare Madame Belle, pretty little Monique and mousy-haired Velma Oakhurst half to death.

Herding them all into the kitchen, Longarm told the pretty quadroon it would be all right to brew some coffee and wake everyone up as he announced, "Neither you nor Madame Belle, here, need to stand trial for murder if you'd be willing to testify against Cora Martin and Miss Velma Oakhurst, here."

The mousy-haired Velma sobbed, "Oh, Mike, how could you say such a thing?"

To which Longarm could only reply, "It was easy. To begin with, I ain't Mormon Mike Mason. I'm U.S. Deputy Marshal Custis Long and we're wasting time whilst the mastermind who got us all into this is getting away."

Smiling wistfully down at Velma, it was easy when a gal was standing there in just her shimmy shirt, Longarm said, "Had you still been over at the boardinghouse with the other innocent bystanders I might have had trouble proving what hit me the moment Davie Glass informed me he hailed from Penn State, the same as you, Miss Velma."

She sobbed, "You can't be serious! I haven't done anything wrong! Since when has it been a crime to stay over at a friend's house?"

Longarm grimaced and said, "You told me she was just a customer, and teched in the head besides. But let's not get into why we found you holed up here. Let's talk about what happened first."

As Monique made coffee with shaking hands, Longarm continued, "What happened first was that a willful young lady from Penn State left home to seek her fortune or, failing that, scout up a maternal uncle, another black sheep of a prim and proper family, who'd already made his fortune out West."

"I don't know who you're talking about!" She sniffed.

He said, "I asked Davie Glass as we were driving in from Golden. I was only half sure until he said his elder sister had married a gent named Oakhurst, from Philadelphia. There's no way your defense lawyer is going to dispute that in court."

She sat down, showing even more thigh, to cover her face with her hands as Longarm went on, relentlessly, "I surmised someone had offered a serious amount for the killing of your uncle as soon as I noticed how tenacious they were about it after Solitaire Stryker had been arrested before he could kill anybody."

She sobbed, "You idiot! You know I have no money! I told you I have no money! Would I be working in that dusty place and boarding in such sordid surroundings if I had any money?"

Longarm nodded pleasantly at Madame Belle to point out, "I'll thank you to note I'm not the one commenting on your housekeeping, ma'am. I'm sure you'll recall I said I was more than satisfied with your hospitality."

He turned back to Velma to say, "I just said you wanted your uncle dead because you had no money of

176

your own. You wanted his. All a single business partner had in the bank along with a half interest in his thriving business. Since you weren't able to pay anything in advance, our Tiger Lady agreed to make a rich heiress out of you for a share in your inheritance. The plan was for all you ladies to sashay up to the town of Golden together, once things cooled down after the killing of your uncle Davie. We know you meant to kill Juan Pablo Jones to cover your tracks as soon as he and Mormon Mike had made you all so rich. So were you fixing to let Tom Corrigan in on it, or was he supposed to meet with some accident here in Brownsville instead of up Denver way?"

"Has anything happened to my Tom?" asked Madame Belle Lasalle in a worried tone.

Billy Vail took over to frankly state, "He's dead, ma'am. Killed by the infernal machine your pal, the Tiger Lady, handed him to deliver. So don't look at me that way. Neither me nor mine ever harmed a hair on his head. He bled to death on the sidewalk when the pal you all are covering up for blew both his legs off at the knees!"

So now Madame Belle was bawling with her head down on the kitchen table and the lawmen assembled drank all of Monique's coffee.

They had the women put more duds on and led them out front in irons to the waiting paddy wagon. They were joined there first by others from the boardinghouse and tearoom, followed a few minutes later by a lean and hungry-looking individual wearing a gray charro suit and matching sombrero, a brace of U.S. Army issue Colt .45s and an uneasy expression.

The *rurale* reported they'd failed to find hide nor hair of La Dama Tigra and demanded to know where they were holding her on their side of the border.

177

One of the rangers was Tex-Mex, able to assure the cuss in fluent working-class Spanish that they hadn't been able to find the *chiflada chingada* either. So the Mex lawman headed back to Matamoros to hunt for her there some more.

Billy Vail ordered the women they'd rounded up held in separate cells at the Brownsville Federal House of Detention. None of the experienced American lawmen argued with him. They all knew how talkative a suspect could get after a night alone, wondering what fellow suspects were up to behind their poor backs.

Leaving the dough they'd kneaded so far some time to rise, Longarm and Billy Vail went back to their waterfront hotel facing the river, chosen for the breezes off the Rio Grande rather than it's not-too-fashionable address.

It was too hot for room service suppers and so Longarm, knowing the current Bronwsville scene better, suggested a sidewalk *cafetín*, as you described a no-frills neighborhood beanery in Border Mex.

As they sat under the woven reed awning with a guttering candle in a *cerveza* bottle betwixt them, washing down cheese enchiladas with iced sangria, Vail sighed and said, "I hope you can see the one who got away is the only one we can charge with murder in the first. That landlady can plead aiding and abetting, even if she refuses to turn states evidence. The colored maid is sure to swear she just worked there and only did as she was told. And she's pretty and only needs one juror to feel sorry for her."

Longarm nodded soberly and said, "I'm way ahead of you. Let's hope we can get a confession implicating Cora Martin out of Velma Oakhurst before it occurs to her that since nobody ever killed her uncle to make her rich, she's only a poor working girl facing modest time for *at-*

tempted conspiracy to commit murder. That Tiger Lady, Cora Martin, is the last of the no-shit killers, now that Stryker, Gleason, Weed, Jones and Tom Corrigan are out of business."

Vail grimaced and said, "You're talking about mere men. That cruel-hearted bitch won't have a lick more trouble recruiting a new gang of gunslicks than she did the last. How do you reckon she manages to hold such sway over men, by screwing them?"

Longarm soberly replied, "She might be a good cook. From the way Madame Belle carried on about Tom Corrigan I'd say he must have been screwing *her*, on occasion. The sex life of the Tiger Lady ain't the question before the house. Capturing the Tiger Lady before she sets up in the same wicked business again is the question before the house!"

Vail inhaled some more enchilada, washed it down, and decided, "She's long gone, south of the border, I fear. We knew the bunch of them liked to work close to the border. Now we know why. With Velma Oakhurst's rich uncle still alive, with her in jail, there'd be nothing holding that two-faced Tiger Lady north of yonder water and we know she can pass for Mex."

Longarm sighed and replied, "When you're right you're right. I don't suppose you'd let me mosey over yonder for just a peek around?"

Vail said, "Not on your tintype and that's an order. I told you on the train coming down that Texas don't care about that bounty hunter shot near here by a person or persons unknown, seeing he was wanted for rape up the river a ways in his own right. But he was a Mex, hunting *hombres* wanted by Mexico on occasion, and I don't want you anywheres near the stomping ground of the late 'Soose Garcia until he's been late a spell longer!"

Longarm allowed that sounded reasonable. Then, as a

familiar figure in a flamenco outfit flounced past, Long-arm sprang up to stride after her, calling, *"¡Hola, La Gitana! ¿Puede darme un momento, por favor?"*

And then as Billy Vail stared after them thunder-ghasted, Longarm and that obvious soiled dove moved arm and arm out of sight into an alley entrance up the way!

"That horny young rascal was on *duty*!" marveled Marshal Billy Vail, adding out loud, "On duty having supper with a superior, least ways! And now he's stuck me with the whole tab!"

Then, to Vail's relief, Longarm returned alone, smiling sheepishly. As he sat back down Vail decided, "Nobody screws that sudden. Couldn't you meet her price, you romantic cuss?"

Longarm said, "We were discussing Mexican politics. *La Gitana*, as we call her. dances in Mexico for fun and whores in Texas for a living. She was the one who told me things about Cora Martin that Cora Martin never wanted me to know. *La Gitana* hadn't heard I wanted to arrest Cora Martin as the Tiger Lady. But working both sides of the border she naturally knows heaps of folk, good, bad or in between, as pals or paying customers."

Vail cut in impatiently, "Swell. Did she tell you where Cora Martin might be at the fucking moment?"

Longarm said, "Not hardly. But she agreed this would be no time for a woman to be riding alone on country roads patrolled by los rurales. So she's likely holed up not too far south of the border with somebody beholden to her. So I asked *La Gitana* to get word to others I know down yonder."

Vail finished his sangria and said, "Even if they find her and even if *los rurales* will give her back to us, prov-ing a capital case without eyewitness testimony or a full confession can be a bitch."

Longarm shrugged and signaled for the bill as he replied, "Let's hope we can get a full confession, then."

Vail laughed wearily and said, "Aw, come on, there wasn't *that* much wine in the sangria and I'm headed back to our hotel for some beauty sleep, seeing we're likely to have a long day ahead of us, come morning."

He was right. They did. Longarm turned in early, himself, and he got more sleep than he'd expected when another squall swept up the estuary to cool the night air a tad.

So he was sound asleep when Billy Vail came pounding on his door at daybreak, excited as all hell about something.

When Longarm wrapped a towel around himself and let him in, Billy Vail chortled, "How did you do it, you whirling wonder? Cora Martin and a Doña Inez just turned themselves in at the border, confessing to murder and throwing themselves on the mercy of American Justice! We have no juristiction over the weeping and wailing Mex woman, but . . ."

Longarm cut in with a smile, "I figured they might. That Vasquez *hacienda* was about as far south of the border as the Tiger Lady would have wanted to risk riding and neither knows they're both innocent of Don Hernan's assassination because I never gunned him for Doña Inez at the behest of La Dama Tigra. I reckon the reason they preferred to come to us was because the late Don Hernan was a personal pal of El Presidente Diaz, a courtly but cruel-natured cuss who's said to like the sounds of screaming."

Vail laughed like hell and said, "We'll have to let the Mex gal go, once she's given us a deposition naming Cora Martin as a well-known professional exterminator. It's too late for either to change stories on us, the two-faced lying bitches!"

Longarm asked, "How come you call 'em liars? Like I said, they still don't know they didn't really have Don Hernan assassinated."

Vail said, "Oh, that ain't what they were lying about this morning at the lockup. They lied about you. You know how she-male suspects are forever trying to compromise arresting officers."

To which Longarm honestly replied, "If that flirty Doña Inez says I kissed her she's full of it."

Vail chuckled fondly and said, "Hell, me and the boys over to the lockup knew that. We all had us a good laugh when first that Madame Belle, then Velma Oakhurst and then Cora Martin charged you'd had your wicked way with them as Mormon Mike!"

Longarm's tone was dryly defensive as he said, "Well, leastways I never got 'round to that pretty upstairs maid."

Vail didn't laugh. But he was smiling as he said, "We figured as much. We might have had us a problem had only *one* she-male suspect accused you. But who ever heard of a lawman taking advantage of three codefendants in one case? We know you ought to be ashamed of your ways with women, you rascal, but nobody could be *that* good!"

182

Watch for

LONGARM AND THE GUNSHOT GANG

274th novel in the exciting LONGARM series
from Jove

Coming in September!

Explore the exciting Old West with one of the men who made it wild!

____LONGARM AND THE NEVADA NYMPHS #240   0-515-12411-7/$4.99
____LONGARM AND THE COLORADO COUNTERFEITER #241
                                              0-515-12437-0/$4.99
____LONGARM GIANT #18: LONGARM AND THE DANISH DAMES
                                              0-515-12435-4/$5.50
____LONGARM AND THE RED-LIGHT LADIES #242   0-515-12450-8/$4.99
____LONGARM AND THE KANSAS JAILBIRD #243   0-515-12468-0/$4.99
____LONGARM AND THE DEVIL'S SISTER #244   0-515-12485-0/$4.99
____LONGARM AND THE VANISHING VIRGIN #245   0-515-12511-3/$4.99
____LONGARM AND THE CURSED CORPSE #246   0-515-12519-9/$4.99
____LONGARM AND THE LADY FROM TOMBSTONE #247
                                              0-515-12533-4/$4.99
____LONGARM AND THE WRONGED WOMAN #248   0-515-12556-3/$4.99
____LONGARM AND THE SHEEP WAR #249   0-515-12572-5/$4.99
____LONGARM AND THE CHAIN GANG WOMEN #250   0-515-12614-4/$4.99
____LONGARM AND THE DIARY OF MADAME VELVET #251
                                              0-515-12660-8/$4.99
____LONGARM AND THE FOUR CORNERS GANG #252   0-515-12687-X/$4.99
____LONGARM IN THE VALLEY OF SIN #253   0-515-12707-8/$4.99
____LONGARM AND THE REDHEAD'S RANSOM #254   0-515-12734-5/$4.99
____LONGARM AND THE MUSTANG MAIDEN #255   0-515-12755-8/$4.99
____LONGARM AND THE DYNAMITE DAMSEL #256   0-515-12770-1/$4.99
____LONGARM AND THE NEVADA BELLY DANCER #257 0-515-12790-6/$4.99
____LONGARM AND THE PISTOLERO PRINCESS #258   0-515-12808-2/$4.99

Prices slightly higher in Canada

Payable by Visa, MC or AMEX only ($10.00 min.), No cash, checks or COD. Shipping & handling:
US/Can. $2.75 for one book, $1.00 for each add'l book; Int'l $5.00 for one book, $1.00 for each
add'l. Call (800) 788-6262 or (201) 933-9292, fax (201) 896-8569 or mail your orders to:

| Penguin Putnam Inc.
P.O. Box 12289, Dept. B
Newark, NJ 07101-5289
Please allow 4-6 weeks for delivery
Foreign and Canadian delivery 6-8 weeks. | Bill my: ☐ Visa ☐ MasterCard ☐ Amex _____ (expires)
Card# _____
Signature _____ |

Bill to:

Name _____

Address _____City _____

State/ZIP _____Daytime Phone # _____

Ship to:

Name _____Book Total $ _____

Address _____Applicable Sales Tax $ _____

City _____Postage & Handling $ _____

State/ZIP _____Total Amount Due $ _____

This offer subject to change without notice.   Ad # 201 (8/00)

JAKE LOGAN
TODAY'S HOTTEST ACTION WESTERN!

☐ SLOCUM AND THE WOLF HUNT #237	0-515-12413-3/$4.99
☐ SLOCUM AND THE BARONESS #238	0-515-12436-2/$4.99
☐ SLOCUM AND THE COMANCHE PRINCESS #239	0-515-12449-4/$4.99
☐ SLOCUM AND THE LIVE OAK BOYS #240	0-515-12467-2/$4.99
☐ SLOCUM AND THE BIG THREE #241	0-515-12484-2/$4.99
☐ SLOCUM AT SCORPION BEND #242	0-515-12510-5/$4.99
☐ SLOCUM AND THE BUFFALO HUNTER #243	0-515-12518-0/$4.99
☐ SLOCUM AND THE YELLOW ROSE OF TEXAS #244	0-515-12532-6/$4.99
☐ SLOCUM AND THE LADY FROM ABILENE #245	0-515-12555-5/$4.99
☐ SLOCUM GIANT: SLOCUM AND THE THREE WIVES	0-515-12569-5/$5.99
☐ SLOCUM AND THE CATTLE KING #246	0-515-12571-7/$4.99
☐ SLOCUM #247: DEAD MAN'S SPURS	0-515-12613-6/$4.99
☐ SLOCUM #248: SHOWDOWN AT SHILOH	0-515-12659-4/$4.99
☐ SLOCUM AND THE KETCHEM GANG #249	0-515-12686-1/$4.99
☐ SLOCUM AND THE JERSEY LILY #250	0-515-12706-X/$4.99
☐ SLOCUM AND THE GAMBLER'S WOMAN #251	0-515-12733-7/$4.99
☐ SLOCUM AND THE GUNRUNNERS #252	0-515-12754-X/$4.99
☐ SLOCUM AND THE NEBRASKA STORM #253	0-515-12769-8/$4.99
☐ SLOCUM #254: SLOCUM'S CLOSE CALL	0-515-12789-2/$4.99
☐ SLOCUM AND THE UNDERTAKER #255	0-515-12807-4/$4.99
☐ SLOCUM AND THE POMO CHIEF #256	0-515-12838-4/$4.99

Prices slightly higher in Canada

Payable by Visa, MC or AMEX only ($10.00 min.), No cash, checks or COD. Shipping & handling:
US/Can. $2.75 for one book, $1.00 for each add'l book; Int'l $5.00 for one book, $1.00 for each
add'l. Call (800) 788-6262 or (201) 933-9292, fax (201) 896-8569 or mail your orders to:

Penguin Putnam Inc.	Bill my: ☐ Visa ☐ MasterCard ☐ Amex _____ (expires)
P.O. Box 12289, Dept. B	Card# _____
Newark, NJ 07101-5289	
Please allow 4-6 weeks for delivery.	Signature _____
Foreign and Canadian delivery 6-8 weeks.	

Bill to:

Name _____

Address _____ City _____

State/ZIP _____ Daytime Phone # _____

Ship to:

Name _____ Book Total $ _____

Address _____ Applicable Sales Tax $ _____

City _____ Postage & Handling $ _____

State/ZIP _____ Total Amount Due $ _____

This offer subject to change without notice. Ad # 202 (8/00)

J. R. ROBERTS
THE
GUNSMITH

___THE GUNSMITH #197: APACHE RAID   0-515-12293-9/$4.99
___THE GUNSMITH #198: THE LADY KILLERS   0-515-12303-X/$4.99
___THE GUNSMITH #199: DENVER DESPERADOES   0-515-12341-2/$4.99
___THE GUNSMITH #200: THE JAMES BOYS   0-515-12357-9/$4.99
___THE GUNSMITH #201: THE GAMBLER   0-515-12373-0/$4.99
___THE GUNSMITH #202: VIGILANTE JUSTICE   0-515-12393-5/$4.99
___THE GUNSMITH #203: DEAD MAN'S BLUFF   0-515-12414-1/$4.99
___THE GUNSMITH #204: WOMEN ON THE RUN   0-515-12438-9/$4.99
___THE GUNSMITH #205: THE GAMBLER'S GIRL   0-515-12451-6/$4.99
___THE GUNSMITH #206: LEGEND OF THE PIASA BIRD
                                                  0-515-12469-9/$4.99
___THE GUNSMITH #207: KANSAS CITY KILLING   0-515-12486-9/$4.99
___THE GUNSMITH #208: THE LAST BOUNTY   0-515-12512-1/$4.99
___THE GUNSMITH #209: DEATH TIMES FIVE   0-515-12520-2/$4.99
___THE GUNSMITH #210: MAXIMILIAN'S TREASURE   0-515-12534-2/$4.99
___THE GUNSMITH #211: SON OF A GUNSMITH   0-515-12557-1/$4.99
___THE GUNSMITH #212: FAMILY FEUD   0-515-12573-3/$4.99
___THE GUNSMITH #213: STRANGLER'S VENDETTA   0-515-12615-2/$4.99
___THE GUNSMITH #214: THE BORTON FAMILY GAME
                                                  0-515-12661-6/$4.99
___THE GUNSMITH #215: SHOWDOWN AT DAYLIGHT 0-515-12688-8/$4.99
___THE GUNSMITH #216: THE MAN FROM PECULIAR   0-515-12708-6/$4.99
___THE GUNSMITH #217: AMBUSH AT BLACK ROCK   0-515-12735-3/$4.99
___THE GUNSMITH #218: THE CLEVELAND CONNECTION
                                                  0-515-12756-6/$4.99
___THE GUNSMITH #219: THE BROTHEL INSPECTOR   0-515-12771-X/$4.99
___THE GUNSMITH #220: END OF THE TRAIL   0-515-12791-4/$4.99
___THE GUNSMITH #221: DANGEROUS BREED   0-515-12809-0/$4.99

Prices slightly higher in Canada

Payable by Visa, MC or AMEX only ($10.00 min.), No cash, checks or COD. Shipping & handling:
US/Can. $2.75 for one book, $1.00 for each add'l book; Int'l $5 00 for one book, $1.00 for each
add'l. Call (800) 788-6262 or (201) 933-9292, fax (201) 896-8569 or mail your orders to:

Penguin Putnam Inc.   Bill my: ❑ Visa ❑ MasterCard ❑ Amex _____ (expires)
P.O. Box 12289, Dept. B
Newark, NJ 07101-5289   Card# _____
Please allow 4-6 weeks for delivery.
Foreign and Canadian delivery 6-8 weeks.   Signature _____

Bill to:
Name _____
Address _____ City _____
State/ZIP _____ Daytime Phone # _____
Ship to:
Name _____ Book Total $ _____
Address _____ Applicable Sales Tax $ _____
City _____ Postage & Handling $ _____
State/ZIP _____ Total Amount Due $ _____

This offer subject to change without notice.   Ad # 206 (8/00)

PENGUIN PUTNAM INC.
Online

Your Internet gateway to a virtual environment with
hundreds of entertaining and enlightening books
from Penguin Putnam Inc.

*While you're there, get the latest buzz on
the best authors and books around—*

Tom Clancy, Patricia Cornwell, W.E.B. Griffin,
Nora Roberts, William Gibson, Robin Cook,
Brian Jacques, Catherine Coulter, Stephen King,
Ken Follett, Terry McMillan, and many more!

**Penguin Putnam Online is located at
http://www.penguinputnam.com**

PENGUIN PUTNAM NEWS

Every month you'll get an inside look at our upcom-
ing books and new features on our site. This is an
ongoing effort to provide you with the most
up-to-date information about
our books and authors.

Subscribe to Penguin Putnam News at
http://www.penguinputnam.com/newsletters

From the creators of Longarm!

BUSHWHACKERS

They were the most brutal gang of cutthroats ever assembled. And during the Civil War, they sought justice outside of the law—paying back every Yankee raid with one of their own. They rode hard, shot straight, and had their way with every willin' woman west of the Mississippi. No man could stop them. No woman could resist them. And no Yankee stood a chance of living when Quantrill's Raiders rode into town...

Win and Joe Coulter became the two most wanted men in the West. And they learned just how sweet—and deadly—revenge could be...

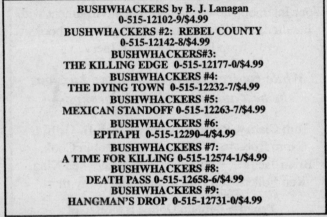

BUSHWHACKERS by B. J. Lanagan
0-515-12102-9/$4.99

BUSHWHACKERS #2: REBEL COUNTY
0-515-12142-8/$4.99

BUSHWHACKERS#3:
THE KILLING EDGE 0-515-12177-0/$4.99

BUSHWHACKERS #4:
THE DYING TOWN 0-515-12232-7/$4.99

BUSHWHACKERS #5:
MEXICAN STANDOFF 0-515-12263-7/$4.99

BUSHWHACKERS #6:
EPITAPH 0-515-12290-4/$4.99

BUSHWHACKERS #7:
A TIME FOR KILLING 0-515-12574-1/$4.99

BUSHWHACKERS #8:
DEATH PASS 0-515-12658-6/$4.99

BUSHWHACKERS #9:
HANGMAN'S DROP 0-515-12731-0/$4.99

Prices slightly higher in Canada

Payable by Visa, MC or AMEX only ($10.00 min.), No cash, checks or COD. Shipping & handling: US/Can. $2.75 for one book, $1.00 for each add'l book; Int'l $5.00 for one book, $1 00 for each add'l. Call (800) 788-6262 or (201) 933-9292, fax (201) 896-8569 or mail your orders to:

Penguin Putnam Inc.
P.O. Box 12289, Dept. B
Newark, NJ 07101-5289
Please allow 4-6 weeks for delivery.
Foreign and Canadian delivery 6-8 weeks.

Bill my: ☐ Visa ☐ MasterCard ☐ Amex _____ (expires)

Card# _____

Signature _____

Bill to:
Name _____
Address _____ City _____
State/ZIP _____ Daytime Phone # _____

Ship to:
Name _____ Book Total $ _____
Address _____ Applicable Sales Tax $ _____
City _____ Postage & Handling $ _____
State/ZIP _____ Total Amount Due $ _____

This offer subject to change without notice.   Ad #Wackers (4/01)